RESILIENT

JIM EWENS

Cover Art By:

Sydney Ewens

DEDICATION

My resilient kids.

CONTENTS

CONTENTS cont'd

THERE'S ALWAYS HOPE

CHAMPIONSHIP

-POST GAME WRAP UP-

ACKNOWLEDGMENTS

Three people have played Major League Baseball with only one hand—that is to say, they did not have two hands that would allow them to play baseball in the traditional way: a glove on one hand for catching and a free hand for throwing.

But they adapted.

This is not specifically a story about any one of them, though I, the author, most definitely drew inspiration from what I consider to be their significant accomplishment.

HOPE & WILL
- A POWERFUL COMBINATION!
ENJOY!

PROLOGUE

Only Now Matters

There was always the hope that future technologies might make Will's life easier. But he wasn't waiting around for them.

He was apt to say, "Only now matters"—and he meant it.

It was 2001.

A ghost from Will's past stood before him, but he didn't flinch. He would take care of this bit of business, and keep moving forward, eyes fixed on the future—the unshakable confidence of a kid who refused to look back.

Lefty

Along with his regular uniform, Will wore an orange compression sleeve on his right arm. He liked how it felt when he was pitching. He used his left forearm to adjust the smooth, silky fabric.

Will's left arm ended at his wrist—where his hand used to be. His hand had been amputated four and a half years earlier—when he was twelve years old.

He took a deep breath, exhaled slowly, and wiped his brow. Beads of sweat trickled down his neck.

It was another scorcher—in the middle of a Mill Valley heatwave.

The last time Will had felt this kind of summer heat was two years earlier, on the day he and his best friend, Mickey, visited the Mill Valley Fair.

Then came the lightning bolt—added motivation.

***

William Orville Williams was just an average kid.

He stood a couple inches shy of six feet tall, though there was little doubt he'd get there—"Growing like a weed," his mom said. He was athletic—good genes had blessed him with a lean, strong physique, already broad across the shoulders. And with his blond hair and blue eyes, all bets were that the word *handsome* would crop up over the next few years.

He wasn't the kind of kid who got himself into a lot of trouble, but being a teenager, trouble had a way of finding him. Though when it did, it tended to be the right kind—and just the right amount.

In fact, at first glance, the only thing outwardly differentiating Will from most of his peers—other than the aforementioned missing body part—were a couple of prominent red scars. One ran through his hairline, crossed his forehead, and cut through his left eyebrow. The other, on his cheek, was a reversed C-shaped mark about the size of a quarter.

Those remnants of deep cuts prompted all kinds of intrusive questions to be directed at Will. If the audience was worthy, he wasn't at all shy about telling the story, but if not, he would casually respond by holding up the middle finger of his right hand and the stump of his left.

Will had been named after his dad's dad, William, and his mom's dad, Orville—affectionately known as Big O.

Now, it's a cruel world that supposes a teenager might have to face high school being both one-handed and an Orville, so Will was really hoping to keep the "O" below the radar.

Another kid in his homeroom ended up drawing some of the attention. That kid's parents, either to preserve a genealogical naming tradition or in a fit of sleep-deprived, new-parent delirium, had named their son Robert. His last name was Loblaw.

When the homeroom teacher called out, "Bob Loblaw," Will knew he was off the hook.

He was more than happy with W.O.W.—he loved his initials, and the nickname "Double Dub" that came with fist bumps in the hallways at Valley View High. That worked just fine.

Another handle—Tank—had been bestowed upon him by his mates on the rugby team, a reflection that once he had the ball, he tended to run people over.

His high school, however, was also home to a dozen or so guys who called Will Lefty.

But to Mickey, his best friend, before and after the accident, he was just Will. Always had been. Always would be.

Will was halfway through seventh grade the day he lost his hand. Then, six months later, he had to start middle school—as a newly minted teenager, no less. With acne.

From the outside looking in, a person might wonder if Will was living under some kind of karmic curse.

Will's instinct was to keep his stump out of sight. *I'll just tuck my arm in my pocket and lay low*, he thought. *Maybe no one will say anything.*

Yeah, right. Middle school offered no such luck. He was the one-handed kid, and he was definitely noticed.

Still, as best he could, he applied a duck-and-cover strategy. Should his mom or Big O ask what he was doing at school, the words *sweet fuck all* may not have been uttered out loud, but they were, most certainly, the only ones to which he could confess.

He muddled through middle school's eighth and ninth grade, somehow earning marks that far overstated the minimal effort he put in. He knew high school was next on the agenda, and he could only imagine the fresh hell awaiting him there. But at least, by then, the end would be in sight.

It wasn't that Will had given up. In fact, under greater scrutiny, it was quite the opposite. From Will's perspective, middle school sucked, high school was going to be worse, and he wanted very little to do with any of it. But outside those middle school walls, by sheer resolve, Will set things in motion destined to pay dividends far beyond his dreams.

And on his life-changing day at the fair, the universe—as it is wont to do—stopped crapping on his head for a minute and lifted the karmic curse.

The lightning bolt came along just at the right time.

That day at the fair was hardly the beginning of Will's battle—he'd been fighting back hard on his own merits. But the universe cranked it up a notch and Will received his just reward for crafting his cloak of resilience and surviving the misery of his amputation.

A week or so after the fair packed up and left Mill Valley, he started high school, and by almost anyone's standards, Will rose to the challenge.

Added motivation can be a wonderful thing.

Sure, he became a bit of a creepy stalker, but that was understandable. He also stepped into the role of defender of the vulnerable, thereby becoming somewhat of a folk hero—albeit one with a black eye and a bloody nose.

Yes, there was the teenage angst integral to tenth grade, but enduring it became nothing more than a badge of honor for Will. And so it wasn't surprising that as eleventh grade, his second year of high school, came to an end, he found himself within striking distance of *those most likely*. He was near the top of the class in English Composition, did just as well in Advanced Math, and, miraculously, he managed to stay awake for almost every history lesson.

And things he set in motion outside of school? Just as impressive.

He became a one-handed force in a dojo and distinguished himself bravely on the baseball diamond.

Which, by the way, was where he was standing at the moment—on the mound, facing one of his tormentors—a ghost from his past. A guy who had rubbed his face in it for over two years. One of those jerks who called him Lefty.

It was high stakes. If he could get this guy out—a monumental *if*—he would walk off the diamond a champion.

You might think Will would wilt under the pressure—but that was a hard no.

Turns out, there was an ember smoldering deep inside Will—always had been. It was a part of him that simply could not be extinguished— by anyone or anything.

When Will chose to fight back from his horrific accident, that ember came to life and started a raging fire of desire.

Which is precisely why Will was the pitcher of choice in the final inning of the championship game. He'd earned the right to be there. It was the culmination of his hard work, optimism, and a belief in himself that defied the odds.

But there is something else you need to know.

Since that afternoon at the fair, someone had taken up a significant portion of Will's attention.

The added motivation in Will's life? Well, that was a girl named Hope.

THE DISARTICULATION

Peach Pie

Twelve-year-old Will was at the dining room table eating breakfast—a stack of books within reach. Joey, his big, black, slobbering dog, was sitting beside him—confident some breakfast remnants would soon be coming his way.

It was a bit before 8:30. Will's mom had already left for work.

His dad was in the kitchen, going off about something.

Something Will had done, done wrong, or not done at all—or maybe it was a school assignment he thought Will "didn't try hard enough on." Really, who could be sure? Will wasn't—he tuned his dad out after his first few words.

He walked in from the kitchen just as Will was about to pack up and head for school.

"For crying out loud, get your ass in gear. What are you doing in here?"

"Homework. What are you doing in here?"

The back of his dad's hand came up quickly, glanced off the side of Will's head, and sent his baseball cap flying—farther than usual.

"That's what I'm doing in here. And you watch your smart mouth."

He was still mumbling as he walked back into the kitchen, grabbed his coffee mug, and headed out into the backyard.

Steeling himself, Will appeared to shrug off the insult and injury. He'd learned to live with his dad's BS—this episode would be buried along with the other "wrongs," but hardly forgotten.

Will loaded up his backpack, grabbed a bagged lunch from the fridge, and took off on his bike, hoping to meet Mickey on the way to school.

The breakfast table event faded from Will's mind as school dragged on. He focused on other things. These were exciting days—a new baseball season was on the horizon. Today was the third practice, and the first game was in a couple of weeks.

The 3:00 bell had barely stopped ringing, and Will was ripping home on his bike. He dropped off his backpack, grabbed his glove and Joey, and headed to practice.

For Will, it was an hour and a half of pure joy. And he was happier yet, hanging around the park after practice, shooting the breeze with his coaches, Mickey, and a couple of the other guys.

Once the gear was packed into the coach's truck, Will gave Mickey a fist bump and told him he'd see him in the morning.

Will was looking forward to getting home. With his dad working late, the prospect it would be just him and his mom having dinner was a welcome proposition.

Will's dad worked Monday to Friday at the mill—morning or afternoon shifts. It hadn't always been that way, but when Will was seven years old, he made a mistake—one that had never been overlooked or forgiven—one that cost his dad a lot of money. That disaster, coupled with the mountain of debt his dad was already drowning in, forced him to take the job at the mill. He kept what little was left of his own enterprise—now nothing more than a side hustle—propped up with weekend jobs.

Of course, Will knew that after the late shift, his dad usually stopped in at Blades Tavern—and that could cause trouble. Often, Will would hear his mom and dad in heated discussions. He couldn't always make out the muffled words they spoke, but the words didn't really matter—the tone said more than words ever could.

It was a lazy ride home from the park for Will. He pedaled slowly as he confided his every thought to Joey running alongside. The bike's chain clicked its easy rotation in symphony with the rusted and rattling fenders. The sun continued its descent into a crimson sky—cotton-candy clouds appeared, hanging motionless against the distant hills.

As they crested the hill just up the road from their house, Will set his cap back on his head. With his hands free, arms outstretched, and shirttails flapping in the wind, he coasted down the grade.

At the bottom of the hill, Joey took a shortcut into the yard. Will turned down the dusty, worn tracks of the driveway, cut across the patchy lawn, and made a jump, thrashing through what was left of the dead and dying greenery lining the front walk.

He hopped off his bike, sent it rolling into the grass, and grabbed the hose. In a few seconds, he was gulping from the cool, clear stream—delicious. Joey drank from the hose too. Will put his thumb over the end, shot a stream into the air, and leaned back as the mist showered down on them.

The sunset was a beauty, but as the vibrant crimson sky faded, the day's warmth disappeared into the dusk. A cool breeze blew across the yard, reminding Will that today was just a hint—the best of spring and summer were yet to come.

Will pulled his baseball glove off the bike's handlebars and wrestled Joey's tennis ball out of his back pocket. He bounced it off the sidewalk, then tossed it to Joey as they headed slowly down the walk.

He took the back stairs two at a time and stepped into the kitchen. The screen door slammed behind him. Joey sat watch on the porch's top step.

"Hey, Mom, I'm home."

The empty kitchen offered a warm hug against the early evening chill. Condensation ran in rivers down the windows. Pot lids danced on the stove. Chicken roasted in the oven. Will's mouth watered.

From another room: "Hi, sweetie. Have a quick wash—dinner's almost ready."

Will walked down the hall to his bedroom. He tossed his glove on the dresser, spun on his heels, and headed to the bathroom. The basin filled as he drank from cupped hands and threw water on his face. The towel held evidence no soap was involved in the exercise.

His mom called to him again: "Sweetie, can you bring your dog in so he doesn't go chasing those darn rabbits?" She also reminded him to set the table.

With the table set, Will took his regular seat, and Joey settled into his strategic spot.

A heavy, cream-colored serving platter was set on the table. Steam rose from roast chicken, mashed potatoes smothered in butter, and peas with early shoots of mint from the garden.

Joey kept his head down and his eyes up.

Will and his mom held hands, closed their eyes, and spoke of that for which they were thankful. This was their ritual when Will's dad was

8

working. Will's mom always said, "Being thankful is what makes a person happy—it isn't the other way around."

"How did practice go?"

"Amazing, Mom! My coach this year is a guy named Raj. He's a super good coach. He promised me I can play catcher this season. Mickey too. So cool to wear all the gear! We can't wait! There! There's something else I'm thankful for!"

His mom smiled.

Between mouthfuls, Will rattled on about how excited he was for the season to start. Every so often, he flicked a couple of peas off his plate to satisfy the beggar at his side—his mom completely unperturbed.

After dinner, Will loaded the plates and cutlery into what they called the magic drawer, then dried the pots and pans his mom washed and set on the counter.

"You go get some homework done quick, and I'll have a treat for you."

Will went to his room, rummaged through his backpack, then headed to the dining room with his books.

His mom assembled a plate of leftovers for her husband and covered it with plastic wrap before putting it in the fridge.

Twenty minutes later, the homework was done.

She ruffled Will's hair as he passed through the kitchen on the way to his room.

Will grabbed a book from his desk and leaned back on the bed. Joey curled up on the carpet.

His mom tapped lightly as she swung the door open, carrying the biggest piece of peach pie Will had ever seen, smothered in melting ice cream.

With bulging eyes, Will professed, "I'm in love."

He put his book away and pulled out his treasure—a shoebox full of old baseball cards—from the desk drawer. He sat at his small desk, scooping up chunks of pie as he thumbed through the cards, studying stats of long-ago retired players.

The shoebox held hundreds of cards, bundled with Velcro straps.

"These are the ordinary ones," his grandpa, Big O, said when he unveiled his gift to Will, "and in this smaller box, you're going to keep *the collectibles*."

Big O had taken great care making the wooden collectibles box. He'd dovetailed the corners and routered a groove across the top of each side panel—a handcrafted lid slid smoothly across the top, keeping everything secure.

Will's cherished collectibles were each encased in a rigid plastic sleeve. The box could hold nineteen cards, but so far, it held only twelve. Will got one of the collectibles each year on his birthday.

He randomly pulled a sleeve out of the box and chuckled as he turned it over in his hands, remembering the special occasion.

Will's dad was working, so Grandpa came over to the house for Will's birthday dinner. They were eating cake when, suddenly, Big O stopped and pretended to search his pockets.

"Oh crap," he said, "I guess I lost a million dollars!"

After a few seconds, he miraculously pulled the plastic sleeve out of his back pocket and slid it across the table to Will as he rattled off the name of a player and a story to go with it.

It was Will's tenth birthday, and he received Al Kaline's rookie card.

"Can you believe it?" Big O said, slapping his thigh. "Kaline joined the Detroit Tigers right out of high school, never played a game in the minor leagues, and spent twenty-two seasons with the team.

"He once played 242 games in a row without making an error—that included the entire 1971 season! I'll tell ya' one thing, that's a sure-fire way to get yourself into the Hall of Fame."

Will remembered his grandpa saying, "Take care of these collectibles. They'll be worth a few more dollars every year. Some of them are worth a fortune now!"

Will looked at his card collection and pondered, *Could baseball cards ever be worth a fortune? How much is a fortune to Big O anyway?*

He figured Grandpa was probably just pulling his leg.

Age Uke

Joey sat waiting, not at all patiently, as the peach pie disappeared.

Will contemplated the melted ice cream, but eventually relented and put the plate down on the carpet. He gave a nod of approval, then watched as the plate was licked halfway across the room.

After sliding the Kaline card back into the collectibles box, Will scooped up the plate, took it to the kitchen, and dropped it in the dishwasher. He poured himself a glass of milk, then wandered down the hall to the living room, with his companion a couple of steps behind.

His mom was sitting on the couch reading. Music played softly in the background.

Will sat down beside her. "What's your book?"

The Housekeeper and the Professor. Yoko Ogawa. She showed him the cover.

"You are definitely going to enjoy reading this after me. It's full of all kinds of baseball and quirky numbers, and it's set in Japan, so that should interest you with your karate and stuff.

"It's a very sweet story, but so sad. Anyway, I'm sure you'll love it."

"For sure. Whatcha listnin' to?" Will asked.

"Well, this is an Academy Award–winning song from 1956. I wasn't even born then, but I just love it—*Que Será, Será (Whatever Will Be, Will Be).*"

Will listened for a moment. "Huh, wondered where it was from. It was on *The Simpsons* a couple of weeks ago. Couldn't get it out of my head the next day—and thanks a lot, Mom, now I'm gonna be stuck with it again!"

His mom laughed. "*The Simpsons,* seriously?"

"My mom used to sing this song to me when I was a little girl. I remember one day we were sitting right there in the dining room. I was only about seven or eight years old."

Oh boy, Will thought. *Here we go.*

It was his mom's thing. She would often say, "There's a funny story about this song," then she'd lead him down some road into the past, pair the song up with a bunch of quirky music trivia, or share a story about what the song meant to her.

"Though I'll pass along to you, something my mom told me.

"She said, 'Sweetie, it's a beautiful song, but thinking 'whatever will be' can be a double-edged sword.'"

"What's that supposed to mean?" Will asked.

Will's mom reflected for a second. "Well, my mom meant life is a tricky thing to figure out sometimes. Sure, it's great to see where life takes you, but at the same time, you don't want to live a life that just happens around you.

"Your grandma was always telling me to take charge—don't wait for fate—create."

"Right. Well, if nothing else, it's a cool bumper sticker," Will teased his mom's words of wisdom.

Then her voice took a more serious tone. "But really, Will, if you don't like what is going on in front of you, do something. Amazing things happen when you step off the sidelines because then you're not letting something happen—you're making something happen. And people take notice of that."

Will gave his mom a hug, then walked down the hall chugging his glass of milk. A fleeting thought about his dad, and the morning, was there and then gone.

Will's mom sat in silence, thinking, *Just be thankful.*

An hour or so later, she opened Will's door. Joey lifted his head off the bed—his tail wagged once. She crossed the room, pushed a lock of Will's hair aside, and kissed his forehead.

"You brushed?" she asked.

"Yup," Will replied.

"See you in the morning, sweetie. It's French toast Friday." She nudged the blankets up around Will's shoulders, then left the room, silently closing the door.

About an hour passed—Will was still awake. He'd just been lying there. Something was bugging him—he wondered if this was going to be one of those Blades-Tavern nights. A few more minutes ticked by, then he heard his dad's van pull across the driveway behind the house.

The kitchen screen door slammed.

Hushed voices. Broken sentences. It wasn't good—Will could tell. Whatever had set his dad off earlier that day hadn't quite been drowned out at Blades.

"Yeah, I had a few beer. So what?"

"And you drove like this? ... this kind of thing? ... teaching your son?"

"...off my back...just more of your fuckin' nagging..."

The accusations went on and were getting louder as Will got up and walked down the hall.

He saw his dad with his pointer and middle fingers extended, poking his mom—first on the shoulder, then again, just below her throat. She stumbled.

Will would never recall moving across the kitchen that night, but he would never forget the sound of him slapping his dad's hand away. Sharp, angry.

There was a blur, and Will ducked instinctively as the back of his dad's hand brushed across the top of his head.

Everyone was still.

"Don't you touch her," Will said.

His dad's hand came up swiftly, on a trajectory to slap him across the face.

Just as swiftly, Will deflected the hand away with an *age-uke*, a rising block—a basic technique Will had practiced at virtually every karate class for the last three years—it was pure reflex.

Again, stillness.

Finally, his dad turned and pushed his way out of the kitchen. The screen door slammed behind him.

"A few beers! That's all! Bullshit family this is..." trailed off as he stomped down into the yard.

Will's mom put her hands on his shoulders. "Go back to your room, Will. I'll talk to him."

Will sat on his bed, clutching his knees. His heart was pounding. His breath ragged. Tears welled up.

Of course, this was not the first time his dad had raised a hand to him, but the swing Will just blocked had real intent. Much like the one in the dining room that morning. Something new had been added.

Usually, his dad would grab him by the scruff of his shirt, threatening a cuff up the side of the head. "I'll knock your block off, Mister," said more to embarrass Will than anything else.

It wasn't always when he'd been drinking, but certainly, over the years, Will learned to take a wide berth—especially when his dad had that smell.

Will heard their voices in the backyard. They grew louder, acid in their tone, then quieter. Then, there was silence.

The kitchen door creaked.

Footsteps in the hall.

Will's door opened slightly.

"Night, Will. Love you."

"Night, Mom. Love you too."

It wasn't the first time Will's dad had come home and made a mess of things, but it was the first time Will stepped in between his dad and mom.

Will didn't know it then, but it would be the last.

Chester & 7th

Will woke to the muffled sounds of dishes being taken out of the cupboard and the sweet smell of French toast emanating from the kitchen.

Hmmm, cinnamon. Definitely worth getting up for, Will thought.

Joey was nowhere to be seen.

He got dressed, then headed, tentatively, to the bathroom.

As he joined his mom in the kitchen, she put an arm around his shoulder—they stepped into the dining room. His mom was quiet as she placed a plate of French toast on the table and laid a kiss on the top of his head.

From his spot, Will noticed a pillow and folded blanket on the living room couch.

"Your dad's already gone," his mom said, "he switched to the early shift this morning—but he wants to talk to you."

Will's forehead creased and he shook his head from side to side.

"You can leave your bike here and I'll drop you at school on my way to work. OK?

"He said he'd pick you up out front a bit after 4:00. He took his car, so keep an eye out for it."

She took a seat across from Will.

Focusing on the cup of coffee in front of her, she bit her lip, then, with glassy eyes, said, "It'll be alright, Will. Talk to your dad and tell him honestly how you feel. I know you have before, and you know it's helped."

She raised her head.

"Something happened to your dad at work and he's struggling with himself right now. This isn't a reflection of how he feels about you or me, it's just that demon he's wrestling with."

A long pause.

"Will, I'm so sorry about last night. Of course, it makes me very sad, but at the same time, I want you to know, I'm very proud of you."

His mom reached across the table, squeezed his hand, then got up and went into the kitchen.

Will finished his breakfast, walked down the hall to his room, and grabbed his backpack.

It was a short drive to school, and they drove most of the way in silence before Will's mom decided to break the ice.

"You know, Will, conflict is funny. Things often get worse just before they get a lot better. It's almost as if we humans get stuck and need a nudge in a new direction."

Will remained silent.

"You know that old *Beatles* song, *Ob-La-Di, Ob-La-Da*?"

"Yeah, I like it," he mumbled.

"Well, there's a funny story about that song.

"When they were in the studio recording it, they had a big fight—John stormed off. A couple of hours later, he came back completely stoned out of his mind. He walked over to the piano and just started slamming the keys. You know, the beginning part?"

"And that's the version they used? Cool." Will was gathering his stuff.

"You got it," his mom replied. "And the moral is?"

"Ah geez, Mom," Will said, as he stepped out of the car.

She leaned toward the passenger-side window. "And the moral is—when conflict arises, it is better to untangle the string than to cut it."

Will crossed his arms on the door frame and leaned in. "Love ya', Mom. Thanks for the lift. And I get it—drugs are OK."

"What? No, I didn't just tell you it's OK to do drugs!"

"Well, it sure sounded like it to me." Will laughed as he turned and headed toward the school.

His mom yelled out the window, "You are such a brat!"

She was smiling as she drove off.

It was hard for Will to focus on anything, with thoughts of the previous night's drama and the pending talk with his dad clouding his mind. The day dragged on.

After school, Mickey hung around with Will. They shot some baskets and talked about the baseball season getting underway. Both agreed they had a great coach and their team was going to "kick some serious butt."

By the time Will's dad showed up, it was about ten minutes after 4:00. There were a couple of other kids hanging around, but the teachers' parking lot had mostly cleared out.

Will's dad pulled his car into the parking lot facing the wrong way. Will got in the backseat behind his dad and rolled down the window.

"Practice tomorrow, Mick. I'll ride over to your place around 9:30 so we can get to the park early."

Mickey stood straddling his bike. "Sounds great."

He waved goodbye, and Will waved back as the car pulled out of the driveway and headed down 7th Avenue.

They drove a couple of blocks in silence. Will was gazing out his window but could sense his dad glancing in the rearview mirror.

"You buckled up back there?"

Will didn't engage.

A short distance later, his dad said, "I have to run into the hardware store for a minute."

He pulled the car over in front of Handy Hardware.

When he came out, he reached through the passenger window and dropped a bag with a thud into the box of stuff sitting on the front seat.

He walked around the rear of the car.

He ran his hand over the minimal tail fins, admiring the aesthetic of his prized possession—a 1965 Mercury Comet Caliente. He had bought the used car shortly after he graduated high school, then spent a couple of years customizing it.

Growing up, Will would listen to his dad tell stories about how he babied his "old beast." He would say how much he used to love driving the cherry-red Merc around town—how he was the envy of all his old high school buddies, especially when he showed up with Will's mom at his side. His dad called those days the prime of his life. Even as a young kid it struck Will, there is some real sadness in those words.

Will didn't know it, but his dad had big plans for his once-pristine set of wheels. He envisioned a day when he and Will would remove the pitted and rusting chrome, spend a few weeks sanding down some blemishes, and do the minor bodywork required to give the Merc a new life. He had long planned to toss Will the keys on his sixteenth birthday.

He stopped at Will's open window.

"About yesterday, Will," he took in a deep breath, and let out a long puff of air. "I want to apologize for both, what happened in the morning, and after I got home from work.

"I know it's no excuse, but I'd been drinking.

"And Will, you did nothing wrong. In fact, I want to say I respect your actions. I really do, and I'm really sorry. It won't happen again."

He opened the driver's door and slid onto the seat. A moment later, they pulled into traffic and headed toward the city center.

Will's mom worked at Safe Harbor Insurance Company at the corner of Chester and 7th. Will and his dad would be passing her office in a minute or so. Will wondered if she was still at work, then he remembered she got off at 3:00 on Fridays, and there was always some kind of special dinner when he got home.

The sun was hanging low on another surprisingly spring-like afternoon.

Will leaned against the door as they drove. He was pitching his hand up and down so it moved like a wave on the ocean, deflecting blasts of cool air onto his face—his hair tousled in the wind.

They were travelling west on 7th Avenue and were about to cross Chester Street when Will's dad glanced in the rearview mirror.

"We'll grab some fries for the ride home, but first, I have to drop this box off at a customer's place. They need it before..."

He wasn't able to finish his sentence.

Will's dad didn't slow down. Why would he? For him, the light was green.

A fully loaded commercial truck was traveling north, approaching the light at Chester and 7th. It didn't slow down either.

Will didn't see it coming, but in a split second, he sensed it.

Darkness.

The impact was absolutely rock solid. To those on the street, the sound was deafening—squealing tires, metal on metal, shattered glass. Absolute violence.

The collision flipped the truck on its side as it sliced through the intersection. It plowed through a bus shelter and into the wall of a bank. A plate glass window exploded into the bank's lobby, another crashed onto the sidewalk and scattered into the street.

Diesel poured from the fuel tank—the stench permeated the air.

After being struck, the car began to spin, looking much like a toy as it rotated clockwise.

For Will, inside the car, there was no sound. Everything moved in slow motion.

The side and front windshield glass shattered into a million crystals. Will's face was pelted.

His head crashed against the car door's frame, then he slammed into the seatback in front of him.

He reached for something to grab hold of, but there was nothing there.

The box from the front seat went airborne and smashed into his cheek.

He thumped hard again into the door—his ribcage taking the brunt of the impact.

After one revolution, the car stopped, and everything was still.

In real time, only a matter of seconds had elapsed, but the severity of the damage done in those moments was indisputable—and things that changed would last a lifetime.

Will didn't immediately react. He sat motionless.

He was cut. That much he knew. And there was tremendous pain in his left arm. His left hand didn't look right, but he couldn't quite recognize exactly what was wrong.

Blood pulsed from his hand—he held it up and watched the blood run down his arm and drip steadily from his elbow.

Blood gushed from his forehead and ran down the bridge of his nose. He could taste it.

Blood oozed from the large gash on his cheek, dribbled down his neck, and soaked the collar of his T-shirt.

He looked down at the steadily dripping blood where it pooled on the white leather seat.

Wonder where that's all coming from? he thought.

The driver's door was folded inside the car—the driver's seat a twisted mess.

The front passenger seat had accordioned in half and pushed the door open. The box from the front seat had vanished.

"Dad?" Will said.

Stump

Suddenly, the rear passenger door was wrenched open. A woman took Will's hand and helped him out of the car.

As he was led away, Will noticed his dad slumped over the front console.

A man from the local electric company hopped out of his service vehicle and peered through the smashed windows. Later, he took a tarp from his truck and draped it over the front of the car.

Will and the woman helping him retreated toward Safe Harbor Insurance, a heavy trail of blood marking their path. The woman's arm was around Will's shoulder. She had draped her scarf over his hand and was supporting his left arm.

Will looked at her and said, "My mom isn't here."

The woman helped Will settle on a front step. She sat beside him, holding him tightly.

An older woman stood at the corner, wringing a handkerchief.

"Oh my Lord, this is so sad. This is absolutely terrible!" she repeated, emphasizing different words each time.

Crowds formed around the intersection. Some couldn't look. Others—the overly curious—milled about, hoping to view the carnage from a more advantageous angle.

As one siren faded to silence, distant sirens grew louder.

Surrounding windows reflected flashing emergency lights.

A paramedic helped Will onto a stretcher. "We're going to take good care of you," she said as she placed a blanket over his shoulders.

Another paramedic held gauze to the top of Will's head, stemming the flow of blood that continued to ooze. A pad was gently wrapped around Will's left hand.

"My mom works in there," he said, motioning behind him, "but I think it's French toast Friday."

"Oh my God. Will?"

The paramedics turned toward a young woman.

"I know him," she explained. "I work with his mom, but she's left for the day. I'll get you her number." She turned and ran back through the insurance company's front door.

A paramedic was speaking to a young policewoman. "Maybe we can save it. Just look around, it could be anywhere—maybe it's lying on the street, or it could be in the car. It's important! Just look."

Will sat on the stretcher. He saw a man point at him, then look back toward the wreckage and explain something to an older cop taking notes of the scene.

Another cop was taking statements from a few other people who had stepped forward as witnesses.

Will's stretcher was loaded into the ambulance. They placed a mask over his nose and mouth.

The siren blared.

Outside the hospital, the stretcher wheels clunked as they hit the ground—he was rolled through automatic doors.

A team of emergency room doctors and nurses swarmed around Will as they prepared to move him onto a gurney.

A chorus of questions and orders—"Is all this blood from his head?" "Let's get his shirt off." "... Mobile X-ray here, quick ..." "We need an MRI ..." "Let's move, people!"

Will's T-shirt was cut off. Sensors were attached to his chest.

A nurse flicked at a syringe, then took his right arm.

Ten minutes. Twenty minutes. Will had long since drifted off.

Will's mom had been called—she was now asking frantically at the admissions desk if they could tell her anything about her son.

An older police officer and his young partner showed up and spoke with her.

An hour passed. She paced the waiting room outside the emergency ward.

Finally, a doctor came and ushered her to a quiet area. Speaking in hushed tones, he explained what they had done, the medications administered, what the X-rays revealed, and what he felt was the best course of action.

The doctor offered support as her knees buckled in reaction to the recommendation that Will's left hand be removed.

The aging and tired doctor explained things with the tact of a bulldozer.

"Every bone in his hand is broken, ma'am. Not just broken—many of them are literally pulverized. One finger was severed completely, and unfortunately, it couldn't be found at the scene. Another is hanging by skin alone.

"Ma'am, we tried.

"Honestly, there is just no way to repair the damage or relieve the excruciating pain your son will be in once those drugs wear off. The sooner we remove the hand and let the plastic surgeon work on the forearm closure, the better off your son will be."

"I understand," she said, sobbing. "OK. OK, go ahead."

"I'll get you to sign some forms," he said. "If you'd please come with me."

The doctor escorted Will's mom to a nurse's station.

He paused and lowered his voice. "Ma'am, I'm very sorry about your husband. My understanding is he did not survive his injuries. I am very sorry for your loss."

***

When Will opened his eyes the next morning, his mom was sitting beside him. She was asleep in a chair, a small pillow propped her head up. She was covered by a thin blue hospital blanket.

Will studied her for a moment. *She's pale*, he thought. *She looks really tired.*

"Mom."

"Sweetie!" she said, taking his hand in both of hers. "You were in an accident, Will, but you're going to be OK." Tears streaked her face. "You're going to be OK, Will."

She pulled his hand to her cheek for just a moment, then stood up, rushed into the hallway, and looked left, then right.

"He's awake!" she called.

"I'll get the doctor," a nurse replied from somewhere down the hall.

A doctor entered the room a few minutes later.

He nodded to Will, then to his mom. "I'm Dr. Mahall. I was with Will last night.

"How are you feeling, Will?"

Will looked at his heavily bandaged left arm. "Fuzzy. My arm kinda hurts. My head too—a lot. And I can hardly breathe."

The doctor grabbed Will's chart, then pulled a visitor's chair close to the bed—across from Will's mom.

"Yes, cracked ribs and a concussion. So, I'm not surprised you've got a headache and I'd expect some blurred vision. You're going to be fuzzy for a while, I'm afraid."

The doctor referred to Will's chart.

"You sustained a deep laceration across your forehead," he said, touching his own forehead to mirror the location of Will's stitches and staples, "and another on your cheek. Though you're lucky—one of our best doctors was here last night and she did a nice job patching you up." The doctor leaned in and closely studied Will's cheek and forehead.

"There's something I have to tell you, Will."

He bowed his head for a second or two, then slowly raised it, pursed his lips, and looked Will square in the eyes.

"We had to remove your hand. It was heavily damaged, and there was no way to save any part of it."

"What?" Will said. "What d'ya mean? But—but that's what's hurting the most. I thought maybe it was wrapped up too tight."

The doctor nodded, explaining to Will and his mom that they had performed a wrist disarticulation, meaning the entire hand had been removed at the wrist joint.

The doctor took Will's left arm, gently squeezing his bicep and forearm.

"The surgery went well, and this feels OK. There wasn't any trauma above the wrist area, and the circulation in your arm appears fine."

He quickly made a note on Will's chart.

The doctor, Will and his mom talked.

Will asked a "what now" question, and the doctor explained what they could expect over the next day or so.

As he scrutinized Will's bandaged arm, he said, "There's a drain under all this—it'll help keep the wound clean. We want to give the whole area a chance to calm down, but one of the nurses will check the incision periodically to make sure all the tissue is viable and everything is as it should be."

The conversation went back and forth.

"So what? I'm going to have a fake hand?" Will asked.

"A prosthetic. Yes, eventually," the doctor replied. "The timing and options are a bit down the road for you, Will. We won't go through any of the fitting process while your wrist area is healing and changing shape, but once we're satisfied with your progress, we can explore all the options. There are a lot out there."

More Q&A, then, as the doctor stood to leave, he asked Will if he'd ever heard of something called phantom pain.

Will shook his head.

"Well, you may sense some itching or burning in your hand—even though your hand isn't there. Let us know if you do—there are treatments."

The doctor referred back to Will's chart.

"For now, rest is the best medicine. We'll be keeping a close eye on you—and your concussion. That was quite a gash on your head."

"How long will he be in here?" Will's mom asked.

The doctor looked at her. "He's going to be our guest for about a week, I'd imagine." Then, turning back to Will, he added, "We'll do what we can to keep you comfortable, and we'll try to make your stay as short as possible. Then you'll be able to go home with your mom."

Before leaving, the doctor said to both Will and his mom, "If you need anything, just let us know."

Once the doctor left the room, Will's mom put a hand on his arm. "Will, I have something to tell you about your dad."

THE BIG MISTAKE

The Shed

It was a simple mistake, a mistake any seven-year-old kid could make.

Though in time, Will would come to realize, from that day, a lot of things started to change at home.

***

Will and his parents had been living in their house for about five years. It was the home Will's mom grew up in. Will's mom and dad bought the property from Big O the summer Will turned two.

The house was creamy yellow with pale green trim. The paint was faded and chipped.

A sidewalk ran from the street to the front steps. Several sections were cracked.

The front and side porches connected and ran along the garden side of the house. Both were in need of repair—spindles were missing from the handrails, nails popped through the aging planks.

The piece of land the house sat on was a little over half an acre and sloped gently from front to back.

There had once been a manicured lawn, though it was now a mix of weeds and stubble in most places and ranged from overgrown to bare dirt in others. The remnants of lawn surrounded a reasonably well-cared-for vegetable garden that had been strategically placed near the shed.

There were a few outcroppings of planted bulbs here and there—they still poked through untended flower beds every spring. Behind the shed, three fruit trees did their best to offer a handful of apples and pears in the fall. Other than that, most of the property had gone completely wild.

On the opposite side of the house from the garden and shed, a dirt driveway ran from the street toward a cracked and worn cement pad. The pad was a leftover from a small garage that had been built at the same time as the house. That building was long gone, and now the driveway turned just before the pad and ran across the back of the house toward the shed.

There was no denying, at first glance, the home and property had a regal appearance, but upon closer scrutiny, it was obvious neither were being given the attention they had once received.

But for a seven-year-old kid, the place was perfect.

Will spent hours in the yard exploring his domain and bravely investigating James McKinnon Park, a greenbelt on the other side of the back fence.

McKinnon Park was part of an acreage bequeathed to the city twenty years earlier after Mr. McKinnon passed away. The city converted his old home into a multipurpose facility, and the remaining land was turned into high-density housing interlaced with a small playground and a plot of community gardens.

After Big O sold his daughter and her husband the house, he moved into a downtown condo. It was viewed by all parties as a great solution. Big O was shutting down his business and downsizing, and the transaction kept the house in the family—which had been his plan all along.

The sale worked well on two fronts for Will's mom and dad—their two-bedroom apartment wasn't meeting their needs, and they had a family business. Will's dad did flooring—carpet, laminate, hardwood, and tile. A graphic of rolls of carpet and the name ON THE LEVEL adorned the side of his work van.

A couple of months after they moved into their new home, they transferred all the business tools and supplies from their cramped storage locker into the comparatively huge shed. This decision saved them a significant expense every month—and fortunately so, because Will's dad was deeply in debt and struggling to dig out of the financial hole his father—his former business partner—left him.

The shed.

Well, they called it the shed, but in reality, it was a fortress. Big O built it himself some fifteen years earlier.

It measured twenty feet wide by twenty-four feet long and did double duty as a garage and workshop. It boasted its own water supply, a small sink for cleaning tools and washing up, and a little woodstove for heat.

In front of the shed's large roll-up door, there was enough space to park two vehicles. That was where Will's dad parked his car and the work van when he had bundles of flooring, rolls of carpet, or whatever else to unload.

Big O wisely put in a regular door on the side of the shed near the garden. It allowed for easy in and out with the lawnmower and gardening tools. To account for the sloping property, he framed in a concrete landing and a nice gentle ramp that ran up into the yard.

***

One Saturday afternoon, after finishing his lunch, Will went outside to ride his bike. He made a little jump on the driveway—all of five inches high—using a couple of bricks and an old fence board. He was determined to get airborne, just like they did on TV.

Will's dad was across town finishing up a job—as self-employment often dictates, it was a regular occurrence on weekends.

Will's mom was in the house doing chores. She would periodically peek out the kitchen window or wave to Will if she stepped onto the porch to shake off a duster.

It was a pleasant summer afternoon, though it looked like a bit of weather might be moving in. Puffy clouds passed by overhead, and trees in the greenbelt swayed in the breeze.

After riding for a while, Will took a break. There was a garter snake nest in some rockery at the bottom of the yard—a constant source of fascination for Will. After a quick investigation, he determined the residents were out, so he opted for some target practice.

He tossed a few rocks at a faded *NO TRESPASSING* sign hanging on a large alder tree in McKinnon Park, then climbed the fence to once again explore the pieces of decommissioned farm equipment abandoned in the bush.

After a few minutes of turning old knobs and trying to budge a seized-up steering wheel, Will climbed back over the fence. He hopped on his bike, did another lap around the house, then rolled over near the garden—looking for his next adventure.

He poked around behind the shed for a couple of minutes and scarfed down a few handfuls of raspberries lining the fence.

Then he noticed the hose lying on the ground. *Time for a drink,* he thought, *and the invention of a new game.* The goal was to see how far he could shoot water into the neighboring yard. He was aiming for a bird feeder hanging in the neighbor's apple tree.

Will's mom popped her head out the door and told him he'd found a good way to earn a talking-to from Mr. Baxter, and instead, it would be helpful if he gave the garden a bit of water.

Will had his thumbs over the end of the hose—spraying a fan of water over the vegetables—when he heard a car pull into the driveway out front. He dropped the hose and ran to see who was calling.

It was his friend Mickey and his dad. Mickey was sitting in the back seat with the window down. He and Will had become best friends after being in the same classroom the previous year.

"Hi, Will. We're going to town to buy a kite. Wanna come?"

With all the joy and excitement that is born in a kid when someone mentions the word *kite,* Will ran up the front steps, threw open the door, and yelled breathlessly to his mom, "Can I go with Mickey and his dad?"

"No problem, sweetie. It's all arranged—I was just talking with Mickey's dad on the phone a few minutes ago. You guys have fun, and we'll see you at dinner," his mom said, walking Will back to the front door and waving.

She stepped down into the yard and passed Mickey's dad a brown paper bag containing half a dozen chocolate chip cookies.

Water

A few minutes after 7:00 that evening, Will's dad pulled his work van down the driveway. He nosed onto the old garage pad, then backed up, pivoting toward the shed.

Been a long day, he thought, *I'll unload in the morning.*

He grabbed his toolkit off the passenger seat, hopped out of the van, and walked across the yard and up the stairs.

He fished his wallet out of the kit, dropped his tools on the porch, let out a long sigh, and stepped into the kitchen.

"I'm home," he said. "Dinner smells good. Where's Will?"

Will's mom was walking into the kitchen. "Pizza and a sleepover. Mickey got a kite, and they were flying it all afternoon. Sounds like they had a great time with that breeze out there.

"How'd your job go?" she added.

Ignoring the question, he said, "His bike is lying out there. He shouldn't just drop his stuff; that's why all his things end up pieces of junk. It could rain tonight, so I'll be talking to him about being without a bike for a few days. We'll see if it smartens him up."

Will's mom remained silent as she dished out portions of pork chops, roasted potatoes, and a variety of vegetables.

Will's dad went to the bathroom to clean up.

After dinner, they tidied the kitchen then sat down for a bit of TV before bed.

The next morning, after their regular toast and coffee, Will's mom left for the grocery store. "I want to get in and out before it gets busy," she said, rushing out the front door.

Will's dad finished up the breakfast dishes, then stepped onto the back porch into a slightly overcast morning. Coffee in hand, he reached down and picked up his toolkit.

Big job starting tomorrow, he thought. *Quick unload, a bit of prep in the shop, then I'll grab some Sunday afternoon R&R.*

He took a sip as he stood on the top step, shrugging off the view of fruit trees that needed pruning and grass, too long in some places and nonexistent in others. To him, those to-dos looked like more work than he would ever have time for.

He stepped down into the yard, walked over to his work van, opened the rear door, and dropped his toolkit in the back.

A slurp of coffee, as he turned and reached for the handle of the shed's roll-up door. It was then he noticed the cement threshold was wet.

Water? he thought.

It was like watching a building collapse in slow motion. He knew what he was seeing and what the impact would be, yet he could not fully grasp an understanding of how the calamity had been manufactured.

He pulled up on the handle, and as the door ran along its tracks, a wave of water flowed freely around his feet, then ran quickly down the slope toward the greenbelt.

Rolls of expensive carpet and underlay, bundles of premium hardwood and laminate, bales of moldings, boxes of tiles, and tools sat in a massive pool—a pool which was now streaming out the overhead door.

In one corner of the shed, he had stored all the thin-set cement and tile grout for his upcoming job. The paper bags and cardboard boxes were soaking wet.

A hundred bundles of flooring stood against the rear wall. He had put them to the side and stood them on end so he'd have room to roll out and pre-cut some of the carpet and underlay.

He stood speechless for a few seconds.

Ruined. was the only thought that crossed his mind.

This was all for a big job he'd landed—a very high-end, eight-unit building in which he was doing every suite, all the hallways, the lobby, and the common areas.

He hustled around to the shed's side door and found the garden hose lying on the ground—running at full blast.

Will left the hose on. He left it running the day before when he went around to the front of the house after hearing a car pull down the driveway. He'd wanted to see who was calling.

The roll-up door, which closed off against the driveway, had a very robust weather seal—commercial grade. Big O's diligence had, over the years, prevented rodents, dirt, and debris from getting in. He was a good builder. He'd built a fortress.

Originally, the side door also had commercial-grade weather stripping. Unfortunately, it was no longer intact. A chunk of a busted cinder block had been used as a doorstop for a few years, and the coming and going tore some of the seal from the bottom of the door.

Big O had installed a four-inch drain and storm grate at the side door when he built the shed, but it was plugged with all manner of leaves and debris that had found its way into the landing over the years—little maintenance.

Still, the drain could accommodate any amount of inclement weather. Unfortunately, there was no way it was ever going to handle the steady stream from the hose. Even an average flow from a garden hose fills a five-gallon pail in under ten minutes.

For over eighteen hours—from Saturday afternoon until Sunday morning—water from the hose ran across seven or eight feet of bare dirt, picking up new debris as it went. Once it found its way down the ramp, it completely overwhelmed the already clogged drain, and there was nothing to prevent it from seeping under the door.

It was absolutely no consolation that some amount of water running into the shed was seeping out through the small gaps around and underneath the big overhead door—because that minimal outflow did little to lessen the massive volume of water pooling inside.

There was thousands and thousands of dollars' worth of inventory soaking in that pool of water. Bought on credit. Uninsured.

It was both immediately and painfully obvious to Will's dad—he would not be showing up at the job site as expected the next morning. He knew it was going to be an uncomfortable conversation with the contractor, and he expected lawyers would be involved.

**

It was mid-morning when Will's mom returned home from shopping.

Mickey's dad dropped Will off about an hour later.

Will's mom and dad were in the shed.

Will walked down the sidewalk. He could hear their voices and wondered what they were doing. He cut across the yard and stopped at the overhead door.

His dad turned and took a step toward him, hands clenched into fists, his face beet red. Spit flew out of his mouth as he shrieked, "You left the hose running, idiot! Go inside and don't come out."

Will's mom stood silent—but only long enough for her to collect her thoughts. "Hey. That is your son you're talking to. My very strong suggestion is that you get yourself under control."

Will glanced further into the shed. He could see the mess—bundles and rolls, bags and boxes, all sopping wet.

His shoulders slumped, and his head hung as he walked dejectedly into the house. He stayed in his room for the rest of the day. He knew it was bad.

Through his open window, Will could hear his parents in the yard.

"Don't you see?" his mom said. "It was an accident. An accident caused by a seven-year-old kid. Yes, he's responsible for this, but do you think you're not?

"If you'd walked over and picked up his bike, you'd have seen the hose running. If I'd come out to the garden, I'd have seen the hose running. If the drain wasn't plugged, the water would have just drained away.

"Lots of things could have gone right, but they didn't. It was an accident, and an accident doesn't make Will a bad kid. He's not an idiot—he's seven!"

Not many more words were spoken in the shed that afternoon. The cleanup proceeded slowly, and once Will's mom and dad had salvaged what little they could, Will's mom went inside. Shortly afterward, Will's dad left, pulling up the driveway in his car.

Will's mom busied herself in the kitchen then carried a plate of sandwiches into Will's room.

"We're having a picnic," she said, setting the plate on the desk. "You sit here, and I'll sit on the bed."

Will's mom put a hand on his knee. "Will, it was a bad mistake, a really bad mistake, but that's all it was—just a mistake."

"I'm sorry," Will said. Tears ran down his cheeks.

"I know you're sorry. And sorry can fix a lot of things, Will, but sometimes it can't fix everything right away."

Will moved to the bed and his mom hugged him around his shoulders.

"One thing I can tell you is this, Will: in your life, you are going to make a hundred mistakes as big as this one—and a couple even bigger," she smiled, "so you have that to look forward to.

"But you are a strong person, and as long as you get up and keep going, keep following your heart, things like this won't be able to hold you back.

"And remember—courage is very powerful against misfortune. Do you know what I mean by that?"

Will looked up at his mom. "I think so. If I'm brave, then something that goes wrong won't be as bad?"

"That's right," she said.

She stood up and walked to the door.

"You know, Will, it's life's challenges that make us resilient.

"You'll say you're sorry to your dad, and we'll all move on. OK?

"You are a good kid, Will."

KIDS DON'T FORGET

Forgotten Lunches

An August sunrise cast a soft glow through Will's window. Will's mom and dad sneaked silently into his room—they placed a cardboard box in his closet. Inside the box was a three-month-old Black Lab.

It was the morning of Will's ninth birthday, and the dog in the box was going to be a complete surprise.

Within a few minutes, Will woke up and pulled his head from under the blankets. In those early moments of waking, all he could do was wonder what the heck was scratching and whining in his closet. He lay there for a minute as he summoned up the nerve to peek inside the door. Once he did, he literally peed in his pajamas.

A head tilted to one side—with a pair of big brown eyes—stared back at him.

With the dog in hot pursuit, Will ran down the hall and into the kitchen. His mom and dad were standing together, laughing their heads off. It was such a great surprise—a great birthday.

"I think it's Joey," Will said as he settled on one of the twenty or so names he'd been considering.

Breakfast was pancakes, and thus began a four-for-Will, one-for-Joey tradition.

They sat together at the breakfast table. Will's mom told him his dad had made all the arrangements. He'd picked the puppy up after work the night before, then stayed with him in the shed, just so Will could enjoy the surprise in the morning.

It was now a month later, and Will's 'great birthday' was most definitely in the past.

Mickey and Will had only been back in school for a short while, though the joys of August were a distant memory.

Mickey stood waiting with his bike at the bottom of Will's front porch.

Will's dad was in the shed, getting some stuff organized for a weekend job he had coming up. The roll-up door was pulled down most of the way—his car and the ON THE LEVEL van were in the driveway.

Will slipped his backpack on, grabbed a dog biscuit out of the cupboard, and tossed it to Joey. He went out the kitchen door into the yard—his bike was leaning against the porch.

"Bye, Dad," he yelled toward the shed as he circled around the back of the house. He wasn't sure if his dad answered or not.

Mickey and Will took off up the street. A short ride later, they cut through a little playground, zipped down a back alley, and were just a couple of minutes from the school grounds.

As they rode the last stretch, they passed alongside a half-dozen kids. They knew one of them—he was in Will and Mickey's class. He was walking with his older brother and some other, bigger kids. As Mickey and Will passed the group, the older brother said something.

The boys pulled up to the school and pushed their bikes through the zigzag gate at the entrance to the playground. As they walked their bikes toward the racks, Will glanced at Mickey. He could see he was upset.

"What's up, Mick?"

"Ah, nothin'. That big kid called me a name. Guy's a jerk."

"What do you mean? What kind of name?" Will turned to see the group they had just passed, entering the school grounds.

"Which one? That guy?" Will said, pointing.

"His brother is in our class—he's been giving me grief every day too."

"Ah geez, Mick."

***

Will's dad finished sorting out the supplies he needed for the weekend.

There were a couple of rolls of carpet and underlay in the work van that were so long they rested on the dashboard and hung out the back door—he decided to use his car for the day.

He grabbed his coffee, pulled down the overhead door, and headed back into the house. Will's lunch was sitting on the counter.

"Will?"

No answer.

Shaking his head, he grabbed Will's lunch and took his own out of the fridge. He took a dog biscuit out of the cupboard and tossed it to Joey, then headed out to his car. He planned on dropping Will's lunch off at school on the way to work.

Tight for time, he thought. *But I should be able to make it.*

Two years had drifted by since he started working at the mill, and it was safe to say, he hated his job more each day—but there were few other options. His business had stumbled, and there was little choice but to take the regular job as a way to dig himself out of his financial hole. Not to mention, having let down a high-profile Mill Valley contractor, his reputation took quite a hit—word traveled fast, and it wasn't long before the jobs dried up.

He pulled up in front of the school and ran Will's lunch into the office. There was a cut-down cardboard box sitting on top of a waist-high supply cabinet, with a sign that read FORGOTTEN LUNCHES. A brown paper bag with a sad face drawing was stapled to the front. A half-dozen bags sat in the box, each one had a name written on it.

Guess my kid isn't the only one, he thought.

He grabbed the felt pen connected to the box by a string, wrote Will's name on the bag, and added it to the six.

The receptionist told him they would announce the names over the PA system and not to worry about Will going hungry.

He checked his watch, thanked the receptionist, then headed out the front door of the school. He spotted Will standing with five or six kids near a basketball hoop, a bit away from the bike racks.

He watched as Will gestured at Mickey, who was standing back a few feet. Mickey was holding both his and Will's bikes. Will was doing most of the talking, directed at two big kids, as a small group started to form. Suddenly, one of the two boys stepped in and shoved Will hard, knocking him to the ground.

A teacher had stopped on the sidewalk in front of the school—she was speaking with a few students. She glanced over in the direction of the group of boys, then excused herself and quickly headed toward the crowd.

Will's dad checked his watch again, saw he was running late, and decided to scoot to his car—he could deal with Will later. Looking back over his shoulder as he opened his door he could see Will still sitting on the ground, looking up at the taller, much heavier kid who shoved him.

He pulled the car away from the curb, and was off to work.

By now, Will had climbed to his feet, taken a quick step toward the big kid, and shoved him hard in the chest. The kid hardly moved. He just stood there, laughing.

The teacher arrived on the scene and told everyone, "Knock it off, or parents will be called!"

"See you after school, ya' little shrimp," the bigger kid said to Will.

"Hey, thanks, Will, but you didn't have to do that," Mickey said as Will grabbed his bike.

"Darn right I did, Mick. You're my best friend."

Dojo

The following Saturday morning, Will was in his room, desperately trying to find two socks—matching or not. Preferably not, was his fashion choice of the moment.

Will's mom was out grocery shopping.

Will was rifling through his drawers, searching under his bed—double-time—but he doubted it was going to be fast enough. His dad had already yelled at him twice to get moving, threatening to "kick his butt" if he didn't get in the car—pronto. He was mad about something, though Will had no idea what it was.

A few minutes later, Will was hopping down the hall, trying to get his found socks on. His dad told him to keep right on going—out the door.

After a short ride, they arrived at the Mill Valley Recreation Center.

This facility was home to a huge swimming pool with water slides and diving boards. There was also a library, a weight room, and on the lower level, there were a few training rooms for yoga, dance and other small classes.

Will had been to the Rec Center before—swimming with his dad a few times when the place first opened and for a couple of weekend-birthday parties with friends from school. But it had been a long time since Will and his dad had been anywhere near this place for any reason, and he had no idea why they were here now.

Since his dad started working at the mill, he hadn't spent much time with Will or taken much interest in anything he did. Will learned it was best to just avoid him.

They walked through the front door and kept going past the library entrance, so that wasn't the reason. No swimsuits or towels—they weren't going swimming, obviously.

Will was kind of walk-running as he tried to keep up with his dad. They passed an information booth without slowing down, then

headed down a flight of stairs and stopped at a door with a sign—
FITNESS ROOM 1.

Will's dad looked down at him. "When I came to drop off your lunch at school the other day, I saw that kid shove you."

Will's face reddened.

"You don't let kids shove you around," he said, wagging a finger in Will's face. "I registered you for this class, and you are coming here every Saturday morning from now on. No questions."

Will understood. He wanted to explain what happened on the playground, but he thought he'd better just keep his mouth shut. Usually, when his dad was mad at him, when he talked to him the way he had, Will just shrugged.

"I'll be back to pick you up in an hour or so. If I'm not here when it's over, just sit tight and wait for me. Got it?" He pulled the door open and nudged Will into the room.

There were mirrors along one wall and a dozen or so chairs along the other. No windows. A man and a kid were pulling some equipment down from a rack at the end of the room. Will recognized the kid. He didn't know his name—he didn't go to Will's school—but he recognized him from playing baseball the previous spring. He was on a different team, but Will remembered his wild orange hair.

Both the man and the kid wore white outfits. The man's had a black belt, and the orange-haired kid's a green belt.

It didn't take a genius to figure out what was going on.

About as nervous as he could be, and not knowing what else to do, Will walked over and sat on one of the chairs. He noticed his reflection in the mirror across the room. He tucked his hands under his legs and kept his head low.

For the next five or ten minutes, groups of parents and kids walked through the door. Some kids were in uniforms sporting white, yellow, orange, or green belts. Others were in street clothes.

Another person with a black belt walked in—a woman.

The kids grouped together in the middle of the room. Their accompanying parents took chairs alongside Will.

The first man with a black belt shouted. "Yame!"

All the kids stopped talking and moving.

"Shugo! Seiretsu!" he barked out orders.

The uniformed kids formed a line across the front of the room. Each belt color stood side by side, facing the mirrors.

Will stayed seated as the woman with a black belt started walking toward him. On the way, she corralled the kids in street clothes, instructing them to fill in the back row.

"You're new in the class today, right? William, is it?"

"Yes, ma'am. Um, Will," Will said softly as he stood up.

"One of your parents registered you this week.

"You're only nine? Wow, big kid!

"OK, well, let's go, buddy boy—I promise we don't bite. Take your shoes and socks off and grab a spot." She pointed to where she wanted Will to fill in.

Just then, the man up front bellowed at two kids fooling around in the front row.

His voice was rough. Scary.

"Hey, you guys, enough!

"You'll be doing push-ups—lots of push-ups!"

Will was really starting to dread whatever it was his dad had gotten him into.

A kid from the second row couldn't contain himself.

"Who you laughing at, Willis?" the man said. His voice had softened. Then a big smile came across his face. Not waiting for an answer, he said, "Excellent! That means we all get to do push-ups.

"Standing bow!"

Most of the kids bowed. Will just stood still.

"And here we go. Ten push-ups!"

As the other kids got down on the ground, Will followed.

"Ichi, ni, san, shi, go, roku, shichi, hachi, kyuu, juu."

Ah, counting, Will thought.

"OK, everybody up! On your feet!

"You in the back," the man was looking at Will, "what's your name?"

"Will."

"Why are you so good at doing push-ups in your very first class?"

"Don't know, sir," Will said softly.

"Maybe it's because you're trying so hard while a few of these other knuckleheads aren't trying hard enough! So, I guess we'd better do ten more—and this time, do them like Will does them."

A few of the kids groaned as they got down on the ground again.

Will followed—with just a little bit of a grin on his face.

As the class was getting back to their feet, the man said, "Reminder—in the dojo, you call me Sensei. Sensei Nic."

He pointed at the woman with a black belt.

"And this is Sensei Carolyn."

"Now, let's break off into our groups. No belts, white belts, and yellow belts with Sensei Carolyn. Everyone else with me.

"First we work, then we play!"

An hour passed. Will spotted his dad sitting on one of the chairs. Other parents had been arriving one or two at a time.

The sensei barked at the class, "Yame. Shugo. Standing bow."

As Will walked over to put on his socks and shoes, his dad stood and approached Sensei Nic. Will kept his head low but watched from the corner of his eye. A brief conversation.

On the drive home, Will's dad said, "I better not see some other kid shoving you around and getting away with it ever again."

Will just kept quiet.

"By the way, the teacher said you did good."

A few minutes later, they pulled down their driveway and parked in front of the shed.

As they were getting out of the car, Will's dad said, "I'm heading out. I've got a job I have to get started on this afternoon."

He pointed at a pile of scrap wood lying on the ground. "While I'm gone, I want you to move all that firewood and stack it inside the shed so the rain doesn't get at it."

"I just need to go inside for a minute," Will said.

His dad's hand came up swiftly and grabbed him by the scruff of his T-shirt. "I just told you what I need you to do."

"I have to go pee real bad."

"Then say that!" his dad barked. "Two minutes, then get out here and get that wood stacked."

Buddha

Will was an eleven-year-old kid, living with a dad who seemed mad at him most of the time—quick to knock his hat off or bark at him—for no reason. Or perhaps there were reasons, but whatever they may have been, they were far beyond Will's comprehension. Either way, Will had a clear grasp of one thing—he wanted to make it stop.

***

Will finished his homework and hurried out through the kitchen door.

His dad was puttering around in the shed. The extension cord was lying on the ground near the mower sitting in some long grass.

Will poked his head through the door and asked, "Is the mower working?"

"Well, it will be once you plug it in and get pushing. What were you doing in there?"

"What I was asked to do."

Will's cap went flying.

"That's the problem with you, Will. You don't listen to me when I'm telling you to do something."

"I listened!" Will yelled. "You said, 'Get your homework done before it starts raining and then start on the grass.' So that's what I did—I finished my homework." Will's eyes welled up with tears as he picked up his cap and turned to leave. "You're just mean!"

"Yeah, and I said don't dawdle over those few homework questions because once the grass gets rained on, it's near impossible to cut, and the job takes twice as long. And you've been sitting in there for over an hour, doing fifteen minutes of homework, and that's just BS!"

Will got the mower started just as raindrops began to fall. A few minutes into his task, he stopped to adjust the height of the wheels—the grass was getting wet, and the mower couldn't cut through the longer patches.

He was still wrestling with the wheel adjusters when his mom called out from the porch, "How long 'til you boys can come in for a snack?"

Will's dad poked his head out of the shed, held up two pieces of something, and indicated they should have been joined together.

"Will should be done with the lawn in about a half hour. I'm working on this, and then I have to head to the hardware store. Shouldn't be gone for too long."

Will figured that meant Blades Tavern.

Forty minutes passed. The ON THE LEVEL van was sitting in the driveway; the car was gone.

In some dark corner of Will's mind, a thought gnawed at him: *There could be trouble later on.*

It was close to an hour before Will finished cutting the lawn. He'd done a decent job on the longer grass—the worn-down patches were hardly worth the effort. He put the mower back in the shed, coiled the extension cord, and hung it in its spot.

Joey chased after the ball a couple of times, then he and Will headed up the back steps and into the kitchen.

"Dad is just so mad at me all the time. He was really mean to me, even though I was just trying to help."

Will's mom stopped wiping the counter and placed both hands on the edge, clenching the dishcloth in her hand. She stood motionless and took a deep breath.

"There's a nice lunch for you," she said, glancing into the dining room. "Finish that up, then you and I can have a talk."

Will sat at the table. It was his favorite—a perfectly grilled green pepper and cheese sandwich. He finished all but the crusts—which Joey was thankful for—then started dipping apple slices into a little ramekin of peanut butter. Every couple of minutes, his hand would go down beside the chair and come back up clean as a whistle.

Will glugged down his glass of milk and took the dishes into the kitchen.

As he and his mom moved into the living room, his mom said, "Will, it wasn't always like this between your dad and me, and it won't always be this way between your dad and you."

They sat on the chesterfield. The incoming weather started to pelt the front window with rain.

"It's tough for your dad. He still struggles with things from nine or ten years ago—things that developed between him and his dad. Your Grandpa William was pretty harsh."

Will's mom was silent for a few moments.

"One day, Grandpa William and your dad had a big fight, and I kind of got stuck in the middle.

"Pretty soon after, that mean old miser shut down their business and left your dad holding the bag—and your dad has been digging out of a big financial mess ever since."

Will's mom seemed to drift off for a second.

"And I guess your dad kind of resents me for that."

"And me too?" Will asked.

"Will, your dad loves you. He just can't seem to get over his anger and shame. His dad broke his heart. He was a mean old man, and most people in town knew it. But he was your dad's dad, and your dad tried to forgive.

"Forgiveness is hard, but I'll tell you something else, Will—forgetting is even harder."

Will looked carefully at his mom. "Every once in a while, he grabs me or knocks my hat off or something, and I don't like it!"

"I know, Will, and I've talked to him about it. I have. I've asked him to see a counselor, and I know he's looked into it.

"I'll talk to him again, OK? It isn't right he does that, and I won't tolerate him being mean to you."

"It doesn't ever really even hurt, it's just, well," Will paused. "I just want him to like me."

"He does like you, Will. It's himself he's not too fond of.

"You know what else I think?

"I think he's embarrassed about how things ended with his dad, and he's disappointed in himself because he didn't see it coming.

"Tell you what, Will—we're both going to have to work on your dad. I think he'll come around, I really do. I know he wants better for you than he had. I know that in my heart.

"Now tell me something, is there any good stuff that goes on between you two?"

"Well, every once in a while, he does something really nice. You know—Joey. And he got me started in karate, which I love, and, well, I notice he works every day just about."

Will's mom smiled. "Thank you, Will. You're a very bright kid."

She put a hand on his knee. "You know, when I was growing up, my dad wasn't perfect either."

"What do you mean?" Will asked.

"Well, for you, Big O is this happy guy who always pulls a sucker out of his pocket, and what you guys have is really special. But when I was a kid, things were changing fast, and those changes created a lot of division in our world.

"Me and my dad didn't always see eye to eye. He'd often say things just to set me off. To him, it was like some kind of joke, and when he saw how mad I got, it only provoked him. It didn't stop me from speaking up, though. You know me—I couldn't just let it happen.

"Thing is, Will, everyone has a movie playing in their head, and in their mind, they're the good guy.

"So, as I say, we have to have the courage to stand up when we see a wrong, but we also have to know, every person is engaged in a battle we know nothing about. Buddha, right?"

"Right," Will answered.

"Ya' know what, Mom? My teacher said something like that once; something about walking a mile in someone else's shoes. I think of that a lot when I'm downtown and see those people living on the street."

WHO ARE THESE GUYS

The Feud

Mill Valley started its transformation from a small town to more of a booming economic centre. It was never going to be a big city, but the lumber industry was called upon to address a housing shortage. All of a sudden, there was money to be made.

At that time, the town most often reflected the mood of a Norman Rockwell painting, though it had its blemishes. A feud developed between two young entrepreneurs—William Sr. and Big O.

It started when they were a couple of businessmen with no kids, but big egos. They got into competitions over business opportunities. It wasn't outright hostility, but rather an unfriendly rivalry simmering in the background. And, as such, it never really threatened to erupt into anything too dramatic

Though it persisted, and years later, though invisible to most people, to Will's mom and dad, it became toxic—the smoke preceding the fire.

The marriage and the birth of a grandson added fuel to the fires, and a couple of years later, things boiled over again, when Big O sold the young family his home.

Still, whatever went on between the two grandpas should have faded away—but it didn't. And once the final salvo was fired, it pushed Grandpa William right over the edge.

Which brings us to karma—the belief that decisions you make send ripples through those around you—even those yet to be.

William Sr. definitely passed on his karma. Will's dad became the next iteration of Williams men to manifest their lacking self-esteem as one round too many, and inappropriate anger toward the people they should have been protecting.

Until the day Will stood up and broke the karmic chain.

Chameleon

There were all kinds of stories about William Sr., the man who was supposed to have been Will's Grandpa William. Some might say he was, biologically speaking, but that was purely semantics.

William Sr. left town when Will was two years old, and prior to that, any time he spent in proximity to his grandson was under duress. The title Grandpa would be a stretch—and indifference would be an understatement.

William Sr.'s quick exit from Mill Valley was just one of his notoriously narcissistic choices, the fallout of which landed squarely on his son's back, pushing him into a fierce battle against a powerful demon.

***

If, as a young kid, Will were to inquire about his dad's side of the family, the answers he received were curiously evasive. Usually, replies from his mom went something like, "He isn't dead, but we'll never see that grandpa again, and all I can say is, I'm not even the slightest bit sorry!"

She once told Will that long before she ever met the man, she heard rumors. And it turned out none of them were far from the truth.

In his darkest days, when the blinds were pulled, William Sr. was a drunk and the kind of guy who smacked his young son around.

He was all of that—and a chameleon to boot.

He promoted his name around town, and, rumored dubious business practices and personality traits aside, he became a prominent figure at Mill Valley's black-tie events. To those in the same business and social circles, his manner of conducting himself didn't seem to matter. In fact, among the upper echelon of Mill Valley, William Sr. was admired as a wealthy real estate wheeler-dealer.

Meanwhile, to the average guy on the street, he was a spiteful and vindictive man. He earned a reputation as someone who could never do a deal and be happy. He always felt the need to get the upper hand—it wasn't good enough to win; the other guy had to lose—and that left people feeling like they'd been ripped off.

In a town the size of Mill Valley, his slumlord reputation spread. Eventually, there were only two groups of people who sought out accommodation in one of his rental units: those who didn't know any better and those without other options.

In the course of building his empire, William Sr. eventually leveraged the youthful naïveté of his son—he suggested a partnership shortly after his kid graduated from high school.

Everything looked rosy when father and son joined forces. William Sr. controlled the purse strings, and his son handled most of the hands-on labor. They would buy an old house, knock off some grunt-work renovations to build up equity, then either resell the property or add it to their pool of rentals.

Sadly, William Sr.'s wife became ill and passed away during this time. This seemed to have something to do with his drinking. It had escalated over the years, but things got even worse once his wife was no longer there as a buffer. He became angrier, more miserly, and ever more belligerent. Even though he had money in the bank—and it was a lot of money—for him, it just never seemed enough.

Even so, the partnership flourished. William Sr. was flawed, but not when it came to being a capitalist.

***

Early one morning the partners were in their office going through some month-end accounting.

William Sr. blew on a cup of coffee as he leaned back and put his feet up on the desk.

"You know what I'd like to see you do?"

"What's that?" his son asked.

"Well, for starters, stop being such a goddamn idiot.

"You've got our partnership—it's stable. Now quit blowing every dime you make on that fancy red car and those big-boy toys. Cars and trucks and boats always end up being worth absolutely nothing. What you should do is get a business going that is yours alone. Something that'll make you a few bucks. I'll take care of things on this side, and you'll reap the benefit of both. Trust me, one day a big payoff will come."

He spun the reasoning, saying it could be a bit of a tax dodge and their accountant could structure things in a way to save them a ton of money.

It was a curious moment, but his son decided to go for it. Over the next few months, he put the finishing touches on his prized possession—his 1965 Mercury. Then he sold his truck and boat, financed a startup business, and soon, ON THE LEVEL was a going concern.

Things went great, and the old man was impressed by the way his son's flooring business integrated into their partnership's real estate activity—especially when the money rolled in.

One would think successful enterprises would be enough to dampen a person's vengeance. In William Sr.'s case, this was not so.

One day, right out of the blue, he told his son not to see Big O's daughter once she came home from college. Said he had to "choose who his family was."

It was a black cloud on the horizon his son didn't see coming—a cloud that brought back painful memories of being treated poorly by an overbearing father, a man who often drank too much.

Those Blue Eyes

Big O played a role in Will's life that couldn't have been more different from that of his future in-law, William Sr.

The history of Orville and how he ended up in Mill Valley was pure fortune.

Long before he became Big O, Orville was in the military and living on the West Coast.

One day, he and a few of his barrack buddies were on a sunny California beach. The football they were tossing around found its way—not so accidentally—into the general proximity of a few bathing beauties.

Oh my.

Orville had just met a gorgeous young woman with freckles and blue eyes—and he proceeded to fall head over heels.

As soon as it was anywhere near appropriate, he begged her to marry him—which she did.

The newlyweds spent a few more years living military life before a palm reading prompted them to leave the West Coast. A few darts on a map dictated a move to Mill Valley.

There, they started a construction business—new builds and renovations—real craftsmanship. It didn't take long to establish a solid reputation among the blue-collar residents of the small town.

It was the '50s, and a young couple with steady jobs could buy a house and raise a family. Orville and his wife made those young families their target market. They did what they could to help them out of rental accommodation and into something they could call their own.

It wasn't long before their business, Big O Construction, was turning a healthy profit—meaning it was time to start a family of their own. Orville became a very proud papa.

Even though he was a quiet man who didn't like to bring attention to himself, from the very beginning, he took a keen interest in his only kid's every adventure.

In the early days, he was Brown Owl to her Brownie pack. It seemed like every weekend, he was setting up a car wash or managing a bottle drive. You could often find him standing in front of a store with half a dozen kids selling boxes of chocolates.

As his daughter got older, he took up the role of coach for her baseball teams. She became a talented player and had no problem playing on what, in those days, were called the boys' teams.

His company sponsored teams and even donated funds for an electronic scoreboard. It was installed just outside the big diamond's center-field fence at Allenby Park. A plywood "THANKS! BIG O CONSTRUCTION" tribute ran across the bottom.

Big O was loving life in Mill Valley—successful business, pillar of the community, wonderful family—and then it all came crashing down when his wife was diagnosed with cancer. She passed away at the tail end of their daughter's first year of high school, only a few months shy of their twenty-fifth wedding anniversary.

Big O and his wife had spent a couple of decades building their business and raising their family with the expectation the golden years would be spent on tropical vacations and doting on grandkids. Naturally, Big O took his wife's death pretty hard.

He kept Big O Construction going for a while, but as time passed, it became evident his heart wasn't in it. Eventually, he wound down the business, sold his daughter and her husband his home, and moved into a downtown condo designed, as the brochure boasted, "for empty nesters." After that, all Big O had on his mind was what showed up on his TV set.

Though it became increasingly clear that a sedentary life wasn't healthy for Big O. He lived in his new home for only a few years before his daughter suggested a move into an independent living facility. It was a great decision.

Independent living was much more to Big O's liking—very quickly he was with like-minded seniors doing seniors' activities, every day. There were trips to the casino, bridge—even poker if he could talk anybody into losing a few dollars.

In the facility's lounge, he spent his afternoons reminiscing about military life to anyone who was interested, or boasting about his grandson Will—whether you were interested or not.

Big O and Will had a special relationship. You could say they became each other's heroes.

In the military, Orville had been a pilot. In Will's early years, he was too young to comprehend the relevance of Grandpa pulling out his medals and walking in the parade each year. Eventually, though, he came to understand—seeing through his young eyes that Big O got a lot of respect from people around town.

But as was true for everyone under a seniors' shared roof, the years were catching up to him. His knees were shot from having worked too many job sites in cold, wet winters, and his memory was going—despite his best efforts to hide it. Though whatever the inevitable signs of aging may have been, the good days still outnumbered the bad.

Over the years, Will and his grandpa enjoyed a lot of quality time together. Will's mom would often bring her dad over to the house for dinner, and as Big O became less mobile, Will and his mom committed to weekly visits with Grandpa.

Those visits became fond memories for Will. Big O was quite a storyteller, and he loved to school his grandson on the quirky aspects of his favorite game.

On one such visit, he rattled off a string of Major League Baseball statistics relative to unassisted triple plays, in comparison to men walking on the moon—a quirky bit of baseball trivia Will was happy to share with Mickey the next day at school. (Ed. note: See epilogue.)

And then there was the accident.

Big O never really talked much about what happened to Will. Then one evening while his daughter was visiting, he said, "Sweetie, Will is gonna be just fine. Heck, he's gonna be better than just fine, he's gonna be every bit as good one-handed as anybody else is with two, you just watch."

Those Blue Eyes II

She had a sick mom at home and missed a lot of her first year of high school. Even so, it's likely Will's future mom and dad crossed paths at Valley View High, though they may never have exchanged a word. Their three-year age gap could have made that prospect unthinkable.

But things change when high school fades into the background and real life takes center stage.

When she graduated from Valley View—Class of '77—she did so with both good marks and a commitment to make her summer before college one to remember.

Some friends already had their driver's licenses and the freedom that went with it. So, a week after graduation, on the July holiday weekend, a dozen kids piled into cars and took off for the lake.

The T-shirts alone—7s Are Wild—were bound to, and did indeed, invite all kinds of attention—spelled 'Trouble.'

The sun was shining, and the water was a shade of blue that barely seemed possible. And he was there, with his big, shiny black truck and a speedboat. He was giving everyone tube rides.

She knew who he was—everybody did.

He had graduated from Valley View the same year she arrived. He'd been a noted athlete with a bit of a bad-boy reputation in the school hallways, and there was no denying he had the rugged good looks to go along with the rep.

She took a couple of turns on the tube, shrieking with laughter as she was whipped back and forth, flying out of control as they crossed the wake.

Later that afternoon, he asked her to stay in the boat and be the spotter.

They got kind of friendly. He was at the wheel, hat on backwards, golden tan, strong shoulders. She sat in the back with the wind blowing her hair all over. Piercing blue eyes, freckles, and a bathing suit—the cut of which her father did not approve.

She would later describe that day as the first time she actually felt like a grown-up.

A week later, she was back at the lake and back in the boat. Before the day was over, they had a something-something going on, and when he suggested a "real date," she was just coy enough to mask her excitement.

The real date turned out to be just that—a real date. A sit-down restaurant, for which he dressed and acted appropriately—holding doors, pulling out chairs, and walking her to the front porch at the end of the night.

She suggested a follow-up, and neither of them could find a reason to stop after that.

It wasn't that she was hypnotized by the trappings of the truck, the boat, and his fancy red car. It was more that, beneath it all, she saw him as an honest, hardworking guy. Yes, he had a veneer, but she was quick to realize it was only there to hide his vulnerability.

She was smitten—and he was the one hypnotized. Those were beautiful blue eyes.

They soon discovered how much they had in common. Both had lost their mothers too early. Their fathers were engaged in similar enterprises. And scary movies at the drive-in were their go-to.

They saw a lot of each other that summer, and it was all bunnies and ice cream. There were more weekends at the lake, and in town, it was Main Street strolls, roller skating, and parking in secluded spots.

He loved cruising down to Kings Drive-In in the evening for milkshakes and fries. With his new girlfriend at his side, driving around town felt even more spectacular.

Then, as summer wound down, reality hit. She headed off to live on campus while attending college in a town called Lumby, about an eight-hour drive from Mill Valley. But that wasn't completely the end of things. He would drive up on long weekends if he wasn't working, and she would return to Mill Valley for the extended holidays.

***

Lumby offered a lot more than Mill Valley, but she chose to hit the books hard and didn't allow herself much of a social life. She was proud to say she was his girlfriend, and when they spent hours on the phone, the talk was all about a future together.

***

Juggling two enterprises was a lot of work, but he stayed focused on the tasks at hand. While his girl was away at school, he chose not to pursue other options. When he was cruising around town, it was usually with his toolbox as company—the work was a welcome distraction.

***

After earning her finance degree, she returned to Mill Valley, and it was only a matter of hours before their relationship was back on—full-time.

They had another spectacular summer together and dated through the following year. A year that included a marriage proposal, a wedding, and an announcement they were expecting.

With a baby on the way, he doubled his efforts with ON THE LEVEL. In many ways, knowing his father's thoughts—regarding his in-laws—pushed him to focus more on his own flooring business and less on the partnership. His dad wasn't always the nicest guy to be around.

And that is when a few dominoes fell.

Domino one was the wedding.

After which, William Sr. pressed his son to put more effort into building up ON THE LEVEL, assuring him he had his back. Which simply was not the case.

There was little time to scrutinize his dad's management, but he believed everything was in safe hands. That was when his father began tilting the accounting of assets and income more heavily in his own favor.

Domino two was Will's birth.

Again, Will's mom and dad tried. Will's given name was his dad's last-ditch effort to build—or at least patch up—some kind of relationship. But it didn't work.

He was busy with partnership responsibilities, his own flooring company, and now had a young family to consider.

Domino three fell when Big O sold the young couple his home.

The optics of the transaction didn't sit well with William Sr.

Meanwhile, he assured his son the partnership was on cruise control, and fair enough, on the surface, everything looked good. But what was lurking underneath was a snake's nest.

Domino four fell the day ON THE LEVEL relocated all its business inventory from a rental unit to the shed.

In William Sr.'s mind, this was tantamount to his son joining forces with his archrival—a move that prompted William Sr. to begin liquidating the partnership—secretively and aggressively.

It's unlikely he planned it from the start, but in the end, when things soured, it got ugly.

It wasn't more than a few months later that he slipped out of town—with not so much as a whisper goodbye.

As time would reveal, the partnership afforded him an opportunity to be creative when it came to managing the finances, division of assets, and tax obligations.

The creativity applied to many of the contracts that William Sr. drew up—structured so that when the partnership finally crumbled, Will's dad didn't receive his fair share. Instead, his father saddled him with significant financial liabilities that would take him years to pay off.

After William Sr. left town, the realization of why things ended, and what his father did weighed heavily, and proved to be a weight that took quite a toll.

LIFE IS WHAT YOU MAKE IT

Sour Cherry Cheesecake

Will and his mom were sitting at the dining room table.

Will was sullen, arms crossed, an empty plate sat in front of him.

"What's going on, Will?"

"What's going on? Really, Mom?"

"What?" she asked.

"Well, OK. Here it is."

He reached over, picked up a jar of pickles, then slammed it down on the table, shouting, "I. Can't. Open. This!

"I'm a twelve-year-old, one-handed freak. My mom has to cut my food for me." Tears welled up in his eyes. "Are you going to floss my teeth too?"

He pounded his fist on the table, shoved his chair back, and stormed down the hall to his room.

An hour or so later, Will's mom opened his bedroom door. She walked in, placed a plate of food on his desk, and took a seat.

"I'm not going to stop," his mom said.

Will was sitting on his bed, clutching his pillow. "Stop what?" Will barked.

"Cutting your food for you. I will very happily keep doing that. I have my son, which is more important to me than anything else in the world.

"Here's the thing, Will. You are different than you were a couple of months ago, no denying it. But that's on the outside. The only person who determines what's on the inside of you, is you.

"And the battle you're in, I'm sorry to say, is going to be a win some-lose some, fight to the finish. But honestly, Will, that's just life."

She paused.

"It's tough, I know, but I'll tell you one more thing, I'm in your corner—and I'm not going anywhere."

She walked out of the room, quietly closing the door behind her.

The jar of pickles was not the first time Will came up hard against the reality of his situation.

Over the weeks and months after his accident, he sank to some very low lows—anger, and shame, and depression, led to a lot of tears. He spent hours alone in his room. He once described life at home to his therapist as "a symphony of slamming doors."

A short while after returning home from the hospital, Will went back to school, which was just plain weird. He didn't have a prosthetic yet, so he kept his arm stump in a shrinker[1] and hidden in his pocket as much as he could—but everybody knew.

Thank goodness for Mickey. Mickey stuck by him, giving him someone to be seen with and opening the door for other people to act somewhat normal—though the reality was, they didn't.

Life at home saw many changes. The Comet was a write-off, and the ON THE LEVEL van disappeared from the driveway. The shed was cleared out.

Will didn't think of his dad often, but when he did, those memories came with a conflicted perspective. The house was suddenly a peaceful place to be, and Will reveled in that, but he also felt sorry for all the things that went wrong for his dad in his short life. Will knew his dad had spent the better part of five years working at a job he didn't like, and that he did so right up until the day he died. And Will recognized that his dad tried hard to keep ON THE LEVEL running as an "I'll show you" to his absent father. Will started to realize how much that must have weighed on him and how that weight pushed him to behave poorly with his drinking and things.

One afternoon, a few months after his accident, Will was standing in the kitchen, silently staring at the fridge. Something new had been added. A baseball schedule was held fast to the door by a few magnets.

---

[1] A shrinker is a tight but breathable compression garment worn over a residual limb after amputation. Its purpose is to: Reduce swelling in the residual limb. Prepare the limb for a prosthesis. Shape the limb for an ideal prosthetic fitting. Maintain limb volume and shape throughout an amputee's life.

His mom was standing at the sink.

"The guy who was going to be your coach, Raj is it? He dropped that off this morning. There's a hat on your desk. He said you're welcome to come by the park anytime you want."

Will let out a puff of air, shook his head, and silently walked down the hall to his room. His door closed quietly.

Will had reluctantly farmed Mickey for updates on the goings-on at Allenby. He missed it—but he didn't really want to know. The realization that baseball was over for him added to his many dark days.

Will didn't take up Coach Raj's offer—not right away at least.

**

One French toast Friday, Will's mom was driving Will to school. She commented that he had missed a big chunk of seventh grade.

"Yup, but it's all good, Mom. It's only elementary school."

"So, nothing special happening today?"

Will chuckled. "Ah, nope. The French toast was pretty much the highlight of my day. From here on it's the same old, same old. Keep my head down, you know."

"Well, then you won't mind skipping out. Maybe head up to the lake? We can grab a couple of subs on the way."

Will turned his head a bit and looked at his mom out of the corner of his eye. "Best freakin' mom ever."

A few weeks later, on a Saturday morning in mid-May, Will's mom sat down at the table and said, "Mickey's dad asked me if I could help him out."

"What's going on?" Will asked, stuffing a fork-full of pancake in his mouth.

"Well, he was halfway through tuning up Mickey's bike when he got a call to go into work. Some kind of emergency. Mickey's bike is in pieces, so he needs a ride to Allenby. His dad will get to the park eventually, but probably not until the game is half over. Game time is 11:00—so I'm leaving pretty soon."

As she stood up, she added, "Do you want to come with me? I'm going to give Mickey a ride to the park, then head downtown."

"Um, I guess so," Will replied. "Will I have to stay? At the game, I mean."

"Totally your call. You can come shopping with me if you want, but if you stay at the park, I can definitely pick you up on my way back."

"Can I bring Joey?"

***

As the teams warmed up, Will leaned against the chain-link fence—on the outside, looking in. Torn. Halfway between first-base and the foul pole—halfway between wanting to be seen and wishing he could disappear.

Joey sat beside him.

As would be expected, the two coaches were occupied with pre-game necessities. One coach, Jesús, was on the field, hitting grounders. The other, Raj, was at the entrance to the dugout, filling in the batting order.

He noticed Will leaning against the fence.

Raj stepped into the dugout, said a few words, then called out, "Hey, Will, can you help me out here? Bring your dog."

Will hesitated for a moment, then took a deep breath and headed over to see what was up.

"Help Mick get the gear on, would ya'?"

A couple of guys high-fived Will as he passed by to the far end of the bench. Mickey was there—turning himself into a pretzel—chasing the straps of his chest protector.

Job done. Mickey hustled out of the dugout.

And sitting at the end of the bench was where you could find Will and Joey for the remainder of the season. They even went with Mickey and his dad when games were played at other diamonds around Mill Valley.

It was great for Will to be at the park, and sure, it was tough to be a spectator, but he didn't dwell too much on the fact a whole season was passing him by. He saw the upside. He was at the park, usually sharing a hot dog with his faithful four-legged companion, and most importantly, those two coaches never let a game go by without saying something to make Will feel like he was part of the team. Life wasn't all bad.

As the season progressed, Will began to think maybe, just maybe, there could be a way to get back on the diamond one day in the future.

***

About a month before Will's birthday, his mom bought him a new bike.

Mickey's dad was one of those guys who could fix anything. He did some research on upper-body amputations and learned how people with that disability stayed mobile on two wheels. Then, over the course of a few weeks, he purchased and installed the necessary components.

First, he fitted Will's bike with a cabling setup that applied both front and rear brakes using only one lever. Then he installed a prosthetic attachment to the handlebars along with a steering damper to make the bike easier for Will to steer. He even found a shift-kit that allowed Will to use all ten gears.

A few days before Will's birthday, Mickey's dad gave the bike a road test, then snuck it over to Will's house and hid it under a tarp in the shed.

On the big day—Will officially became a teenager—Mickey and his dad rode over to Will's for a birthday celebration. The boys manned the BBQ, and everyone sat at the picnic table in the side yard, eating burgers and hot dogs. The big black slobbering dog was both an absolute pest—and handsomely rewarded for being so.

After enduring the worst rendition of Happy Birthday ever, a huge sour-cherry cheesecake was devoured, and the bike was rolled out of the shed.

Will's initial response was tepid—to Will it looked like a bike for a kid that couldn't ride a bike—but Mickey's dad pointed out the custom features, and his enthusiasm became contagious—Will finally broke into a smile.

Mickey stayed for a sleepover, and the next day, Will pushed the bike up to the front street, hopped on, and he and Mickey took off. Once Will got moving, he was all smiles. His mom's intuition was right—the bike quickly became Will's independence.

Kids Like Me

A week after his birthday, Will entered middle school as a thirteen-year-old. Again, he relied on his good friend Mickey, and Mickey stuck with him through all of it.

Middle school teenagers. Perfect. A whole new crop of people checking out the one-handed kid.

Though it hadn't seemed remotely possible to Will, things went from "not great" to "completely screwed up" when, on day one, a kid in the hall uttered the first "Lefty."

Proof that Will thinking *Things could be worse,* wasn't a sliver of optimism—it was actually a prediction.

The kid's name was Brad, and he was about as classic a jerk as you'd find on every *ABC Afterschool Special.*

From the first day, Brad and a few of his buddies looked for every opportunity to get under Will's skin. Antics like plunking themselves down at Mickey and Will's table in the cafeteria.

"So, tell me, Lefty, does your mommy do up your zippers for you? All of them?

"I call him Lefty because his left hand left, and his right hand is all that's left. That's a lot of lefts, right, Lefty?"

All Mickey and Will could do was move to another table, though Mickey was happy to leave a few parting words. "Tell me something, Brad—do you even know you're an idiot?"

Brad was at least a couple of inches taller than Will and heavier. He had brawn and power. Will, still growing into himself, was lean and more suited for speed and endurance. And while Will was understandably a bit withdrawn, Brad was just the opposite.

From their first meeting, Brad quickly sensed his advantages over Will. It seemed to be his mission to make Will's life miserable, taunting him with Lefty this and Lefty that, while throwing in a few "scar-face" jabs for good measure. They were just words, but there was an unsaid challenge lurking below the surface.

There weren't many days when distractions took the focus off the one-handed kid, and things never did get much better for Will. All he could do was try to avoid Brad and his buddies, though it wasn't easy.

Will signed up for the track club and the chess team—endeavors Brad was never going to be involved in. And after mastering the mechanics of his new bike, he secured a paper route.

Fall became winter, then winter gave way to spring. As the days got longer, another baseball season's preparations got underway. Mickey was at the park a lot, prompting Will to consider his options. Only a year had passed since the accident, and Will didn't know if he could play, but he sure wanted to try. He lobbied his therapists and his mom, but after lengthy discussions, the idea was taken off the table.

"Give it one more year," seemed to be the standard answer to his begging.

Raj had drafted Mickey to be on his team again, and Will was invited to hang out as he had the previous year. His love for spending time at the park untempered by the fact he was a spectator only.

It was early in the season, and Will had been at the park for every practice and game, so Raj figured he'd open the door.

Jesús was running infield drills—Will was chasing balls that got through the gaps.

Raj was showing kids the proper setup at first base if they were intending to steal second.

He watched Will for a few seconds and made a decision. *The kid's got heart, and he makes himself useful—at least he's not hangin' around here like a hair on a biscuit—think I'll get him up on the mound and see what he can do.*

He called out to Will with some words of encouragement. "Hey, Will, why don't ya' grab a bucket of balls and throw a few?"

Before Will muttered more than two words of an "I'm-not-allowed-to..." or "I-don't-have..." excuse, Raj barked at him, "Hey! Did I say anything about what you're allowed to do, or what you don't have? No! So get your butt up there and start throwin'!"

After practice Raj said to Will, "Just tell your mom I said you could practice with the team."

For that limited level of involvement, Will's mom gave her OK.

"Nope, not playing, Mom, just throwing the ball around a little bit," Will lied over dinner.

Almost true—Will was just throwing the ball a bit, and the results were kind of spectacular.

From the first time Will got up on the mound, Raj saw something. From then on he took Will through the basics of the cobra grip[2], how he was going to hang the cape[3], even though he had his glove cradled on his stump and continually drilled him on the importance of striding down the mound[4].

It soon became clear, Will had some natural ability.

The season ended, and another summer came and went. Will and Mickey, now fourteen-year-olds, entered ninth grade, their final year of middle school.

During the Christmas break that year, Will and his mom visited Big O at the independent living facility for a special dinner.

Big O asked Will what he was doing at school. "Sweet fu...—ah...um" Will bit his tongue, then opted to go with "Shakespeare," knowing it was sure to be a conversation killer.

Then Will quickly changed the subject, telling Big O he was in the top ten in the school's Running Club.

"Well, sure you are. One thing about you, Will, ya' always try so darn hard. Not surprised you're one of the fastest kids on the track."

On the drive home, Will's mom said, "He's right, you know. You've got something not everyone is blessed with."

"What's that?" Will asked.

"You're an optimist, and I can prove it!" his mom replied.

"Oh really?" Will said. "How so?"

She glanced over. "Well, tell me three things that are kind of important in your life right now."

---

[2] The Cobra Grip or four-seam grip provides straight carry to the target.

[3] During a two-handed pitcher's windup, their pitching hand and glove hand are extended as if they were 'hanging a cape' Dracula-style. Will couldn't do that but Raj coached him how to achieve some extension between his pitching hand and his glove.

[4] The foot in contact with the pitcher's rubber is known as the push foot. It propels the pitcher 'down the mound.' The further down the mound the stride, the more momentum is built when the pitcher pivots on his landing foot, adding velocity to the pitch.

Will pondered for a few seconds, then said, "Mickey—my one and only friend—the guy is saving my butt at school. And there's the skateboard you're gonna let me buy. And the obvious fact middle school is almost over!"

"Bam! And there it is," she said. "Thankful for something, looking forward to something, and putting something in the rearview mirror.

"Optimist, Will. Total optimist."

It was absolutely true, Will was an optimist—and a thinker.

The downtime offered by the Christmas break gave him a window to reflect on things. Obviously, expressing indifference to his situation was a challenge, but over time, he realized being a one-handed kid didn't bother him as much as it made other people uncomfortable.

It struck him that people became weird once they saw his disability. He knew why—they just didn't know how to react, or what to say. Will considered it might help his situation if he took the responsibility to change that.

Sitting in the safe haven of his bedroom, Will resolved to forgive the outside world and just be the best he could be.

They don't know about kids like me. He thought. *They think I can't do anything. But they just don't know.*

I'm pretty sure I'll be able to play baseball again somehow. Maybe next year in high school, I'll be a track star, I mean, I know I can run! And they play rugby at Valley View which just might satisfy my burning desire to knock someone on their ass.

He chuckled at thoughts rattling around in his head. *I'll just try it all; whatever I can do one-handed. And if it ain't sports, whatever, I've got my brain as backup!*

Will didn't know exactly what his future would look like, but if nothing else, he had chosen a direction—forward. And that was enough for now.

And once Will went looking for them, he did find glimmers of hope scattered through the day-to-day drudgery of a new calendar year. He got the relative amount of independence associated with being a teenager. His paper route enabled him to bankroll some of his own desires—he was loving his new skateboard. And other than schoolwork, the things he did, he did with the kind of resolve that ensured no one could say he wasn't trying.

A Bronze Memory

On a Saturday morning, a couple of weeks into the new year, Will was sitting alone in his room. It was just a bit after 8:00. He'd gotten up early and eaten breakfast with his mom, who was now out grocery shopping.

Will sat at his desk, conscientiously procrastinating his to-do list. Joey was curled up beside him.

Will was studying a pristine collectible card, marveling at the statistics of a player named Willie Mays. Another guy who never played a game in the minors.

Will figured Mays' story was one in a million.

The card told how Mays went one for twenty-five at the plate to start his major league career. Granted, his only hit was a home run—even so, his slow start could have foretold a very short stay in the majors.

But Mays wasn't that kind of guy. He kept at it—he knew he wasn't a one for twenty-five hitter. By the time the season ended, he was hitting .274 with 20 home runs—that is around seven hits out of every twenty-five at bats. And he walked away with the Rookie of the Year award.

Will figured there was probably some kind of lesson in there about not giving up.

He put the Mays collectible back and sat quietly at his desk. He glanced up at the half dozen karate medals hanging on his bookshelf—they prompted a memory from his time at the dojo.

***

The Saturday morning Will's dad dropped him off wasn't exactly a great introduction to karate, but after navigating the first few lessons, the idea of not going to class never entered Will's mind.

With his dad working most weekends, Will's mom took up the cause, driving him to the rec center on Saturday mornings. Will enjoyed the stuff he learned—not just the physical aspects, but also the history and meaning of the katas.

And Will really took to his senseis. They praised him for his hard work, and if he wasn't quite getting it, they were always there with words of encouragement.

"Hey, Will, just remember the three most important things. You want to be good at karate—or anything else, for that matter—all you have to do is practice, practice, practice."

That mindset rubbed off on Will—he practiced—and after only his second term at the dojo, he was awarded his yellow belt.

He was so proud to become a full-fledged member of the club—a karateka.

On his tenth birthday, he unwrapped a brand-new gi.

***

One of Will's medals was attached to a piece of braided green ribbon. Will stared at it and chuckled. He remembered the day he walked into his first karate tournament—an environment completely foreign to him.

It was a Sunday morning in late October, about six weeks after Will returned to the dojo for the fall session—with his shiny new yellow belt—and a gi in which he was practically swimming.

Will and his mom drove to South Bend High School and pulled into a parking lot plastered with signs: *Golden Rule Dojo Karate Tournament – Sunday 9:00–5:00. Public Welcome.*

They parked and followed other parents and kids heading toward the entrance.

Will looked at his mom as they walked into the gym.

"Yikes," she said.

Chaos.

There were about two hundred spectators in the stands, tables of organizers and judges were spaced all around the gym, and karateka were buzzing everywhere.

Even a local TV station had cameras set up on the stage.

Sensei Carolyn materialized, corralled Will, and took him to a warm-up area. Kids of all ages were doing kata techniques. Will just stood there—it was a whirlwind, and his head was spinning.

Fifteen minutes later, Will and some other kids were marshaled back to the gym and led to one of the three competition mats. When he spotted his mom waving at him from the stands, all he could think was, *Geez Mom, be cool, please!*

The speakers blared, "Now on mat number two, we have the Boys Eleven-and-Under Kata, Novice Division."

Will leaned forward and looked up and down the row of competitors kneeling on the mat's edge—a mix of four yellow belts and three white belts.

Great, Will thought. *I've been ten years old for all of two months, so I'm probably at the bottom of the age category too.*

A white belt knelt beside Will—the kid was huge. The yellow belt kneeling on the other side of Will had a big number three on his sleeve.

"Pretty new yellow belt," Three-on-the-sleeve said as he looked down at Will.

"Just got it," Will replied.

"I got mine over a year ago," Three-on-the-sleeve said.

"Nice. What's the three for?"

"That's how long I've been training. Three years."

Will gulped.

A name was called, and the kid at the far end of the row stood up, bowed, and walked to the middle of the mat. He called out a kata name, then went through steps, punches, and blocks. Once he finished his routine, he bowed and stood motionless, hands clenched in front of him.

Judges at each corner of the mat held up numbers, grading the kata demonstration.

The second kid in Will's group was called. He had a white belt. Then the third kid, a yellow belt, went up. Then Will's name boomed from the speakers.

***

Will's mom had her arm around his shoulder as they walked across the parking lot.

"You must be so proud," she said, "winning a medal in your very first tournament. That'll be a great thing to show your friends at school."

Will's face was beaming. "I couldn't believe it when they called my name—is this gold?"

"You won bronze, sweetie, which is really good!" his mom said. "What were you thinking when you were up there? How did you even know what to do?"

"Honestly, Mom, I didn't have a clue what was going on! I figured I'd just do the one kata I'm kinda good at and try to do it the best I could."

Lesson from my kid, she thought. *If you got dressed up to be someplace, then stand up and do what you know, and do it the best you can. That's all anyone is expecting of you.*

In another tournament just before Christmas, Will entered his first kumite competition. Sparring was new to him, and he loved it.

On the way home, his mom dropped him off at Mickey's.

"So, was it pretty or ugly?" Mickey asked, eager to find out if Will had won another medal.

"Actually, it was both," Will said. "Got my butt whooped by some eleven-year-old freak of nature, and I don't really want to talk about it."

When Will showed up at his next class, Sensei Nic took him aside for a quick chat.

"It's all good, Will, because now we know what we need to work on. And we will. The Valentine's Day Massacre is in two months, and you'll be fighting again."

The outcome of that competition was more to Will's liking.

On the drive home, he opened and closed his hand over a gold medal as his mom took what seemed to be the long way home.

And all he could think was, *I want more.*

Shodan

And Will did win more.

Though his three years of practicing karate came to a dramatic end the day he lost his hand. March 14, 1997.

***

Will was still sitting at his desk, looking at the gold, silver, and bronze medals dangling from the shelf.

Now the memories were coming fast and furious—one, from a class about a month before his accident, flooded over him.

At the beginning of the class, Sensei Nic spoke to the karateka assembled in their rows and the parents watching.

"I want to tell you all something that is unique about karate.

"I think you would agree, everyone who starts taking karate has a vision of one day earning their shodan, their black belt, right?"

Kids and parents nodded their heads.

"Well, let me tell you something. Honestly, it is extremely hard to earn your shodan, and it saddens me to say not everybody here will get that far in their practice."

Sensei scanned the dojo, noticing many raised eyebrows.

"But I'll tell you something else.

"It is one hundred percent true that no matter who you are, where you come from, or what kind of challenges you have in your life, once you start taking karate, you are guaranteed to get a black belt, as long as you do one thing."

Sensei looked left and right.

"Now, does anyone here know what the one thing is?"

"Practice, practice, practice!" a kid blurted out.

Sensei chuckled. "Well, yes, but no."

He waited.

"If you guys don't get it right, we'll have to do some push-ups."

Will raised his hand as a couple of other kids shouted out answers.

70

Sensei pointed. "How about you, Will? Any idea what the one thing you have to do is?"

"Um," Will hesitated for a second. "Keep coming to class? I mean, like, just don't quit."

Sensei burst out laughing. "Oh, my goodness! I got the right answer! Maybe I should retire!

"That's right—just don't quit. Just keep showing up, and one day, you will get a black belt. There is literally nothing that can stop it from happening.

"I know it sounds easy, but it's hard to do!

"OK. So now we don't *have* to do push-ups. Instead, we *get* to do push-ups! Everybody down.

"Ichi, ni, san, shi..."

***

"I wonder," Will said, barely loud enough to disturb Joey's morning nap.

Within a few minutes, Will was on his bike. By 9:10, he was standing at the locked door of FITNESS ROOM 1. The Saturday morning class started at 9:30, and Will had raced to the dojo, hoping to catch Sensei Nic before anyone else was around.

Some second thoughts.

He turned and looked at the stairs, then back at the door—here he was, fourteen years old, standing there, wondering if he was out of his mind.

Then Sensei Nic called his name.

"Will! Great to see you," he said, coming down the stairs.

"Come on in." He unlocked the door. "Booker stopped to return some books, but he'll be down in a few minutes. Are you just dropping by?"

Sensei bowed as he entered the dojo. Will did the same.

Will's stomach sank as the dojo flooded him with emotions—an essence in the room that spoke to Will's three years of training—training that had ended so abruptly.

"Well, not exactly," Will replied as he kicked his shoes off and quickly removed his socks.

"So, what's up? I haven't seen you for quite a while. I was thinking the other day I should check in and see what's going on. Is everything OK, Will?"

Sensei slipped out of his shoes and hung his jacket on a coat rack.

Will tossed his jacket onto a chair.

"Yeah, everything's fine, I just, um, well," Will stammered, "I was wondering if it would be allowed for me to still try and learn karate, all things considered." He held up the stump of his left arm.

Sensei took a step back and studied Will. "My goodness, you are about the bravest kid I ever met."

Not waiting for Will to respond, he continued, "Do me a favor, Will."

Sensei was tying his faded and worn obi around his waist. Japanese characters embroidered in gold thread adorned each end.

"Do you remember your han zenkutsu-dachi? Your fighting stance?"

Will stepped back with his right foot, his feet shoulder-width apart. The toes of both feet were turned in slightly. He held the stump of his left arm in front of him—his left hand would have been about chest high. His right hand was clenched into a fist just above his right hip, corkscrewed slightly to its right.

"Good stance," he said as he looked Will up and down. "Now, step and punch. Head up. Watch my eyes. Strong punch. Right here." He patted the stomach area of his gi.

Sensei stood about four feet in front of Will—his feet square, shoulder-width apart.

Will stepped and punched. His fist was short of making contact by about a foot.

"Good, good. And again," Sensei said. "You've still got pretty good form, Will!"

Will stepped back into his stance and repeated the technique.

After a few iterations, Sensei moved in a bit closer.

"Again, fighting stance. Step and punch. Head up. Strong punch. Right here." He patted his stomach—then clenched his hands into fists and rested them on his hips.

Will stepped and delivered a good, strong punch. It slapped into Sensei's gi, making a sound like someone fluffing up a pillow.

"Again. Strong now, with a *kiai!*"

Will complied.

"And again," Sensei said. .

But before Will threw his next punch, Sensei moved one half step closer.

OK, Will thought. *This guy could snap me like a twig, but he asked for it, so here goes.*

Will expected to land his strike right in Sensei's midsection, but the blow never arrived at the target.

As Will delivered his punch, Sensei swung his left elbow—sharply deflecting Will's fist. In a split second, he stepped his right leg in behind Will's right leg and brought his right forearm up with force, catching Will square across the chest.

Will's momentum carried him forward at the same time the forearm to the chest stopped him cold. He was about to get knocked on his butt—helpless—until Sensei grabbed his shoulder to steady him.

Sensei's left fist was still on his hip. It hadn't moved.

"Is that what you want to learn?" he asked. "How to defend and attack without using your left hand?"

"Yeah! Can I?" Will asked.

"*Tai sabaki*. Whole-body movement. You turn, shift, or pivot—to avoid an attack. You better your position and create an advantage.

"Instead of meeting force with force, *tai sabaki* helps you redirect, dodge, or angle away from an opponent's attack while staying balanced and ready to counter.

"And when you counter, *enpi* strikes are incredibly powerful," he said, touching his elbow and winking at Will.

"The object is to create space.

"Space gives you time, Will, and time gives you the opportunity to think.

"And I'll tell you something right now—if there was ever a kid who could master these techniques, it's you."

Will smiled as his face turned red.

"OK, look. I think I've got an idea—I'm going to call your mom and talk to her about this, OK? Does she know you came down here this morning?"

"Um, no," Will replied. "I wanted to ask you if it was even something I could do first and then see if it was gonna be OK with her.

"It's one of those delicate questions—'Mom, can I do it, and, uh, can you pay for it?'—if you know what I mean. But I'm doing a paper route a couple of days a week, so I've got some money."

"I get it," Sensei said.

"Hey, before you go, do you have any extracurriculars on Tuesday and Thursday afternoons?"

"Just my papers," Will said, "but I finish around 4:30. I do them right after school."

Just then, Sensei's son Booker came through the door. There were fist bumps all around. After a quick chat, Will took off and headed over to Mickey's.

A few hours later, he cruised down the hill toward home.

His mom was prepping dinner.

"Hi, Will. Gyoza tonight," she said as he stepped into the kitchen.

"Take Joey out for a bit, OK? He's been missing you all day."

Later, at the table, Will was doing his impersonation of a starving wolf.

His mom asked, "How many of those things can you eat?"

"Is 'more' a number?" Will was heading back to the kitchen.

"I talked to your sensei today," she paused, "you are quite a kid, Will."

Will sat down at the table again. "Did I do something wrong?"

"Not at all," another pause. "Sensei was asking if, after your papers on Tuesdays and Thursdays, you would help him with the kids' class."

"Like, help him how?" Will asked.

"Teaching kids the basics is what he said to me on the phone."

"Seriously? That'd be so cool!" Will said.

"He's got a proposition for you. If you help out in the dojo, you can train as much as you like—no charge."

Are You Left Handed

Will's mom woke him early.

"There are a couple of things I'd like you to get done if you want to hang out with Mickey this afternoon."

Will got out of bed, brushed his teeth, and followed his nose to the table.

"What things?" he asked, knowing Saturday morning chores took priority.

His mom pointed to the stack of pancakes and bacon sitting in front of him. "Go easy. One and one for him, OK?" She nodded at Joey.

"And when you're finished your breakfast, I'd like you to sweep the side and front porches and the sidewalk up to the street. And if you could blitz the yard, that would be great.

"And then," she said, standing with her hands on the back of the chair across the table from Will, "I'm taking you down to Jackson's to buy a new glove. You want to play this year, right?"

Will's plate of pancakes and bacon disappeared, and he was out in the yard within minutes.

There was no warmth in the late-February Saturday morning sun, but it shone brightly—a brief respite from the dreary days that enveloped Mill Valley the previous month.

When you're sweeping with one hand and a prosthetic attachment, it's tough to be all that effective, but as was true in most cases, Will sucked it up and did his best.

Joey made the rounds, and Will alternated between tossing a ball for him and focusing on the assigned tasks.

With the porch and sidewalk spruced up, Will took a tour of the yard.

The ground frost was a thin lace veil over the dormant vegetable garden. Remnant leaves, blown in from somewhere, crunched under his feet. He walked the property, picking up the gifts Joey had left for him during the week—most of them harmlessly freeze-dried, though today's was still worthy of being held at arm's length.

Once the morning's chores—along with the bomb disposal, and a bit more ball throwing—were complete, Will opened the back door and called out to his mom, "All done."

Ten minutes later, they were in the car.

"You haven't eaten in what, three hours?" his mom said as she pulled into a drive-through.

"Way overdue," Will replied.

"All right, Will, name it and claim it."

"Old Fashioned Plain and a Honey Dip, please," Will leaned over and called out through the driver's side window.

"Make it two Old Fashioned Plain, a Honey Dip, and a small black coffee. Please and thank you," Will's mom added.

"And a tea. Loaded. Please and thank you," Will finished off the order.

As they were exiting the drive-through, Will's mom suggested, "How about a little *Chumbawamba*?"

"I'm singing the chorus!" Will replied.

Drinks and donuts in hand, together they belted out *Tubthumping* as they drove toward town.

A few minutes later, they pulled into an almost empty parking lot. As the cooling engine clicked and pinged, Will's mom turned and said, "I'm proud of you, Will." She nodded at the dashboard's CD player.

The lyrics rang true in both of their minds.

"Yup," Will replied.

They sat outside the tired three-story brick building—drinks were finished and donut crumbs swept to the floor.

Jackson Brothers Department Store was a fixture in Mill Valley. It sold almost everything: ready-to-assemble furniture, clothing, housewares, and all kinds of hardware.

The basement was home to an outdoor section stocked with gardening supplies, camping equipment, and sporting gear.

It was the go-to place for beginners, but there was a decent selection of middle-of-the-road equipment and even boasted some high-end stuff too.

Will browsed the baseball gear, checking the mid-range gloves, occasionally looking up at the models sitting on wall racks or hanging on the hooks above. There the gloves were illuminated by the store's display lights. Those were some nice gloves.

Since his dad had died, Will knew there wasn't a lot of money to be spent on extras, as his mom called them. With his fingers crossed, he scanned the price tags dangling from above, but he knew he would not be picking from the racks and hooks—not at those prices.

He strolled off to the side where there were a couple of tables piled high with gloves, jocks, and batting helmets. With spring around the corner a whole new contingent of younger kids would be gearing up for the season.

Will started digging through the piles but quickly realized this display was home to baseball gloves in name only. Not all of them were little kids' sizes, but those that weren't were on the very low end of any baseball-glove-quality scale.

A store employee passed by.

"These are pretty middle of the road," he said, "but you might find a couple in there that are better than the others."

Will's mom tracked Will through the sports section, looking up at the hooks and racks, biting her lip as she saw the price tags.

Who's paying a hundred and twenty-five dollars for a kid's baseball glove? she thought, shaking her head.

She approached Will at the tables. "Anything here look OK?"

Will silently glanced back at the higher-end gloves, then at his mom, and continued digging.

After a minute or so, he pulled a right-hand glove up from the bottom of the pile. It didn't have a price tag, but it was obviously a better glove than most of the others.

Rawlings Genuine Hide Leather Deep Pocket Double Stitching Pro-Elite Model embossed in gold ran across the pocket and along the palm edges.

"How much, sweetie?" Will's mom asked, seeing he'd found something of interest.

Will shrugged. "No price tag."

Will's mom took the glove and walked over to the cash desk.

"Do you know how much this glove is?" she asked.

The employee had a MANAGER tag on his chest pocket.

"Oh yeah, this one," he said, taking the glove and turning it over in his hands.

Will followed his mom but hung back a bit.

"It's a model from last year. It was a return. Someone bought a right-hand glove because their kid is right-handed," the manager chuckled. "Guess they don't know much about baseball, huh? It's a good glove, though."

He looked at Will. "Are you left-handed?"

Will was standing with his arm stump and right hand in his jacket pockets. He pulled his left arm free. "Sort of limited options now."

The manager quickly looked back at Will's mom.

"It's a really good glove—I think it was around eighty dollars brand new last season." He scratched the side of his head as he glanced at Will, then back at his mom.

"No tags on it, and it's been out of the store. I think the kid even tried to use it in a game," he continued scratching.

"Look, we don't sell a ton of right-hand gloves. That's why it's still sitting there.

"Tell you what—final sale, thirty-five bucks?"

"Thank you very much," Will's mom said, pulling the bills out of her wallet.

Will was clutching the glove to his chest as they walked out of the store and hopped into the car.

Will's mom said, "I think I better hit the gas. That was a steal!"

Will laughed. "It's a super nice glove, Mom. Big O gave me a Brooks Robinson baseball card and a poster for my birthday one year. He used a Rawlings glove too!"

The thumping of Will's stump in the glove's pocket continued for the entire ride home.

Within minutes, Will dug a bottle of leather conditioner out from under the kitchen sink and sat in his room, applying it to his new glove.

He opened the bottom drawer of his dresser, pulled out his old baseball glove, and retrieved the softball from the pocket. He tucked the ball into the pocket of his new glove and tied the glove up tight with a shoelace—then he set the right-hand glove beside his old left-hand glove on top of his dresser.

He stood looking at the two of them for a few seconds, shrugged, then headed down the hall toward the kitchen.

"I'm riding over to Mickey's, Mom."

The screen door slammed.

***

The yard was still an unkempt cacophony of long grass, dead grass, and no grass, which made it the go-to spot for pitching and batting practice, dog training, and every other diversion that kept Will out of the house.

In the days following his purchase, Will was in the yard every chance he got.

Practicing with his new glove became an obsession. He'd cradle the glove on his arm stump, toss the ball up in the air, and try to get his hand into the glove in time to make a catch. Though it was tricky, he soon mastered the toss-in-the-air-and-catch routine.

There was scar tissue along the wrist area where the surgeon removed Will's hand, and even two years after the surgery, if he used it too much, it could get sore. But he stuck to it, and as his level of proficiency elevated, so did the practice routines.

Magnifying Glass

Joey was watching his every move.

As Will angled the lens, a beam of light fell sharply focused on the glove. A trail of smoke snaked into nothingness in the light afternoon breeze. Within a few minutes, scorched initials ran along the glove's thumb edge.

"Wow," he proclaimed.

He'd been sitting on the porch for a while when his mom stepped through the kitchen door carrying two glasses of lemonade.

"Love my initials," he said.

After his mom sat down, Will proceeded with a verbal documentary on some research he'd been doing.

"I read up on these three guys, Mom—Peter Gray, Jim Abbott, and Chad something . . . Bentz, I think it is. All of 'em played Major League Baseball one-handed, and two of 'em were pitchers!"

"Seriously? That's pretty amazing." Will's mom was as surprised as she was impressed.

"Yeah, Gray lost his right hand in an accident, like me, but Abbott and Bentz were actually born without a right hand. Well, without one that would let 'em use a glove the regular way, at least.

"It's crazy how well they did. Abbott played ten years in the majors, mostly in the American League, so he didn't have to bat. Designated hitter, right?

"But listen to this, Mom." Will could hardly contain his excitement. "That Peter Gray guy? In his first game playing semi-pro ball, he went up to bat with two outs and the bases loaded in the bottom of the ninth. The guy hit a walk-off line drive, and the fans threw money on the field for him—around seven hundred dollars! That was a lot of money in 1942, right?"

"Darn right it was! There was a war going on, and things were tough."

"And guess what, Mom? In 1945, he made it to the majors with the St. Louis Browns. He played in seventy-seven games and got fifty-one hits. Two of them were triples!"

Will was shaking his head.

"And Bentz! He grew up in Alaska, for crying out loud! How does a guy with one hand get to the majors from Alaska?"

"Well, probably by doing just what you're doing," his mom answered.

Of course, Will's mom knew more about baseball than most moms. She'd been a good ballplayer herself, and now that Will's return to the game was imminent, he rarely stopped talking about old players, stats, and rules.

"Well, I know there's nothing wrong with your noggin, so show me your ball stuff."

Will stared at his mom. "Well, that's just creepy."

"Gross!" his mom yelled, punching him on the shoulder.

Will was laughing as he jumped up, grabbed one of the lacrosse balls littering the yard, and went to a worn-out patch of lawn. He cradled his glove on his arm stump, then threw the ball hard so it skipped off the ground, ricocheted against the side of the shed, and came back about chest high. The ball slapped with a thud into his mitt.

"See? I'm totally getting the hang of it."

"Wow, you really are getting good!"

Will had done his research. He'd figured out that by cradling the glove on his arm stump, secured against his body, with the finger holes facing down toward his wrist, once he threw the ball, he could slide his hand into the glove and be ready to make a catch.

He'd been at it for a couple of weeks. The first few attempts looked more like self-preservation, with Will dodging the returning ball more often than he caught it. But the process evolved into a competition. He managed to get to ten in a row. Then twenty. One day he did over a hundred, and after that, he just did it without counting.

His mom watched as Will demonstrated a few more times.

"You think you'll be OK to play this year?"

"Totally. Any spot they want to put me, I'll be a happy camper. But last year, Raj had me on the mound at practice, and I actually think I could pitch in a real game.

"Heck, Jim Abbott only has one hand, and six years ago, he pitched a no-hitter for the Yankees! September 4, 1993."

"You're sounding more and more like Grandpa all the time!" his mom said.

She stood up from the steps, walked down into the yard, and gave Will a hug. After ruffling his hair, she turned and headed back inside, picking up the empty lemonade glasses as she went.

***

Will improvised a target using a wooden apple box stuffed with some old carpet underlay. He set the box on a white plastic lawn chair and stood it over near the fence.

Then he practiced the process over and over—skip the lacrosse ball off the dirt, field it as it rebounds off the shed, transfer the glove back to the crook of his arm, fish the ball out of the pocket, and make a throw to his lawn-chair target.

Of course, the continuation of that process was to gather up the balls that had gone flying all over the place.

One day, Mr. Baxter, Will's neighbor, was out mowing his lawn. He took a break and watched for a few minutes, peering over the fence as Will went through his routine.

"Very impressive, Will!"

Over time, Will's accuracy greatly improved, which was a good thing on the neighbor front because the fence boards had taken a beating. His improvement, however, shifted the burden to the apple box, and it wasn't long before the remains of the chair and a pile of kindling lay in the grass—a testament to Will's determination.

One evening, Will arrived home from his dojo, parked his bike, and ran up the back steps.

"Did you see what's in the yard?" he asked his mom as he stepped into the kitchen.

"Mr. Baxter. He's pretty impressed with your progress."

Will grabbed his glove and ran back outside.

The bits and pieces of the apple box and chair were gone. They had been replaced by a four-foot by four-foot pipe frame, secured to a base with six-inch wheels. Netting was stretched tightly around the frame, with a thick fluorescent-yarn rectangle woven at the center. If you hit the rectangle, the balls dropped into a catch bag—it was a perfect target—sturdy and mobile.

It was getting dark when Will's mom finally convinced him to come inside for dinner.

***

Mickey was a good friend; he never said anything weird about Will's missing hand.

When he didn't have something going on at the pool, he was usually over at Will's. They'd fire grounders and throw pop-ups to each other.

They also stepped off a home-to-second distance so Mickey could practice his pickoffs. Mickey did the same thing that Will did—ricochet the lacrosse ball off the shed, then fire it to Will standing at a makeshift second base, and Will would lay down the tag.

They did bunting practice and used a bag full of wiffle balls so Will could swing away one-handed. The balls rattled into the net target for hours.

One Saturday afternoon the boys got creative.

Mickey held the end of a big tape measure as he walked.

"Right there, Mick," Will called out.

Mickey put down a piece of plywood about the size of a home plate where he stood, and Will hammered a makeshift pitcher's rubber into the grass where he was standing.

"Sixty feet, six inches from the rubber to the plate—Big O once told me the story of how it came to be." Will chuckled as he added under his breath, "Might even be true."

Will's mom brought the boys iced teas, and they took a break—sitting on the porch steps, Mickey leaned back on his elbows.

"Nervous at all?"

"A little," Will said. "I've never played on the big diamond."

"It's different for sure, but even for a guy who's taken two years off, I think you're doing great. I mean, seriously, Will, I catch for other guys, and trust me, by comparison, you've got a freakin' cannon."

"Well, I just want to play—anywhere really. It'd be great if we were both on Raj's team this year, because I think he'd let me pitch a few times."

"Oh, pfft, you're gonna be on the mound for someone, and I'm gonna paint a target in my catcher's glove. Ya' hit the mitt, ya' win a prize—just as if you're picking off duck targets at the fair!" Mickey mimicked himself holding a rifle.

Diamonds

There were enough kids registered for the 1999 season that it allowed Mill Valley's Baseball Executive to build four teams in the fourteen-to sixteen-year-old age bracket.

The Saturday morning draft got going, and the four coaches picked their top choices. Brad went early—every coach knew he was a big hitter.

Raj picked Mickey in his first rotation.

On the second rotation, with Mickey safely on his lineup, Raj chose Will over some more sought-after players—a move, which under different circumstances would have surprised the other coaches. The truth was, Raj had suggested it was a good idea to keep Mickey and Will together—he didn't get any pushback at all. No one seemed in any hurry to get stuck with the one-handed kid.

But Raj knew exactly what he was doing. He recognized a few things about Will. He knew the kid really wanted to play—and he'd spent some time with him at practices the year before. He also knew, as good as Will was, he was committed to getting better—every time Will stepped on the mound he proved the point.

So, almost as if it were scripted, Will was heading back to Allenby on the same team as Mickey with Raj as coach.

A week before the season started, at a Sunday afternoon session, Raj walked out to the mound. Will was getting ready to throw batting practice—Mickey was behind the plate, donning his catcher's gear.

"You're ready for a real game next weekend, right? I know you've been chomping at the bit," Raj said.

"Absolutely, Coach. I'm super excited!" Will answered.

"You seem to be pretty good at that one-handed throw-and-catch thing," Raj said, nodding at Will's right-hand glove.

"Yup, Coach, I think I got it. Been working on it a lot, actually."

Raj chuckled. "Figured you would.

"Well, Will, I wanna share a couple of my thoughts with ya'."

Raj leaned over and grabbed a worn baseball out of the bucket. He picked at the seams with his thumb as he spoke.

"I don't want ya' to freak out, but I'm gonna ease ya' into things for the first few games, OK?"

Will's brow furrowed just a little.

"But make no mistake, Will, I'll be fair. And trust me, you are gonna be pitchin' this year."

"Cool!" Will said.

"But here is the thing. I've seen a lot of pitchers your age, and I can tell you a bunch of 'em looked like they were gonna be quite something for a little while. Then, as time went on, they turned out to be not-so-much-of-anythin'.

"So, I'm gonna be careful with ya'. I don't want you to fizzle out—and I don't think you will.

"Pitchin'? For you, it's in your blood. And ya' know what else? It's clear to me whatever is in that arm of yours starts off in your head, which makes you a rare commodity.

"You're a diamond, Will." Raj poked him in the chest.

"I really love it, Coach," Will was beaming.

"Great. Well, I'll keep tellin' you how, and you just keep tryin' your best. OK?"

A week later the season got underway, and a funny thing happened on the day Will returned to Allenby—in a game that mattered.

Opening Day games were scheduled on all the fields at the park. There were little kids on the small field playing their first game of T-ball, right up to Will's division on the big diamond, and every age group in between.

As the baseball gods decreed, Will's and Brad's teams were slated to play each other in the second game of the day—the other two teams faced off in the morning.

By the time the afternoon match-up got underway, there was a larger than usual crowd of parents and kids hanging around the park.

Coach Raj's lineup had Will playing right field starting in the top of the third inning. Raj was strategically taking all the pressure off Will.

So Will and Joey grabbed a spot at the far end of the dugout and waited.

Will had also checked the batting order. His name was right at the bottom of the list.

"Don't worry, Will. You're my secret weapon," Raj said when he saw Will let out a sigh.

Will's team managed to get a few runners on base early in the game, and Will was "in the hole" when the third out was recorded in the bottom of the second inning.

At the top of the third, Will jogged out to right field.

The ball didn't come his way once, but he didn't care one bit. He was just happy to have the grass beneath his feet. After the third out, he jogged in, knowing he was on deck.

"This ought to be good," he said to Mickey as he grabbed a bat from the rack. "I can only guess what he's going to say."

It didn't take long to find out.

The leadoff batter hit a weak grounder on the second pitch and quit running halfway to first base. Then Will stepped out of the on-deck circle and walked toward home plate. True to form, Brad, who was playing third base, threw out a taunt loud enough for everyone to hear.

"Hey, Will, you batting right-handed or right-handed?"

Fortunately, Brad's attempt to throw Will off came to a screeching halt—two things happened.

It was as if Coach Raj was waiting for it.

"Time!" he called as he began a purposefully slow walk from his spot just outside the dugout. He passed behind the umpire—pausing to say, "Gimme a minute here, Blue"—and strolled over toward the other dugout.

Some of those on the field and in the stands were just now learning about or seeing Will's left arm. Others knew the story very well.

There was an immediate hush in the crowd as the other coach stepped up to meet Raj. But before he did, he turned, and in a voice even louder than Brad's said, "Hey, knock it off!"

The two coaches, old friends, chatted for a minute, shook hands, and patted each other on the back. Then Raj made the slow walk back. "Good luck, Will," and "Thanks, Blue," as he passed behind the plate.

Now, the "knock it off" alone may not have been enough to shut Brad up. But the other thing that happened was, on the second pitch, Will laid down a perfect bunt. The ball rolled lazily down the line toward third base, where Brad was standing—flat-footed.

For the next twenty seconds, Will's teammates went absolutely nuts in the dugout.

Brad fielded the ball late and forced a wild throw to first base—his throw ended up rolling to the fence behind the bag. Will took the turn at first and just kept running. He was already rounding second by the time the right fielder retrieved the ball. That guy had the good sense to throw the ball to the pitcher instead of trying to pick Will off as he slid into third.

Brad and his coach had a few words behind their dugout between innings—words that went something like, "...and that's why you don't mouth off to other players! Because after you do, they have a habit of scoring runs on you!"

Brad was silenced for the remainder of the season.

True to his word, Raj used Will every game—creatively and strategically. He cycled Will between right field, first base, and the mound.

During practices and in games, he taught Will much more than just how to throw. His lessons also included the mental part of the game.

One day, after a tough loss, Mickey and Will were helping Raj load up the gear.

Raj stopped for a minute and turned to Will.

"Heck, Will, I know you could probably knock a peanut off a fence post. And sure, it's that, but pitching isn't just about how well you can throw the ball—there's a whole lot more to it.

"I get it, it's your first year back, and honestly you're doing really well. But I'm not about to let you develop a bunch of bad habits, so listen up."

Raj rested his foot on the bumper of his truck.

"You wanna win close games like this? You gotta be smart. And I know you are—problem is, today, that's all you were.

"See, bein' smart and thinkin' ain't the same—and ya' gotta do both if ya' wanna be a pitcher. Otherwise, you're just a thrower."

Raj turned toward Mickey.

"This conversation goes for you too, Mick. You and Will are a team out there.

"Together, you guys gotta figure out what a batter is likely to do. Swing for the fence or just go for contact. And that tells ya' what to throw at 'em—and when. That's the key.

"And it ain't just the batter. A pitcher has an awareness of what is goin' on all around 'em. Where are they in the order, does the count allow 'em to waste one, is a base runner taking too big a lead?

"That's what I'm talkin' about."

Raj picked up a heavy equipment bag and tossed it in the back of his truck.

"You guys wanna know the difference between a thrower and a pitcher? I'll tell ya', throwers throw and pitchers win.

"Trust me, guys, one day Will's gonna be staring down the barrel of some kid he has a history with. That's when it becomes much more than just strikes and balls. Ya' gotta think your way out of that predicament—that goes for both of ya'."

Oh yeah, Raj was full of lessons, and Will and Mickey were keen to take them in.

Once the season wrapped up, the boys said goodbye to middle school and did what most fourteen going on fifteen-year-old kids did during the summer—as much nothing as possible.

Will's nothing, however, was frequently interrupted by chores around the house.

One day he would be dripping with sweat as he wrestled the mower up and down the side yard. The next he'd have tools and hardware scattered on the porch, tackling repairs to the stairs and railings.

Tending the garden was an every-summer-day occurrence, though it would be a lie to say Will was anything other than forced labor. What was true, was the more he helped his mom out, the more he saw the connection between planting, tending, harvesting, and his favorite part—eating the fruits of their labor.

He came to recognize the time he spent outside was a meditation.

On sunny summer afternoons, Will pondered his one-handed future. This always brought a certain resolution to his mind. He realized both Sensei and Raj were right—work first, play second—and think. Even his mom's words of wisdom factored in—make it happen.

And the proof was, his hard work did make things happen, on the diamond, and in the dojo. He also recognized his get-up-again way of thinking meant he was spending a lot less time on his ass than he, at one time, thought he would.

So, he figured, I'll do more of what I'm doing.

One afternoon, Will was coiling up the hose. He paused, noticing how the garden glistened like diamonds in the late afternoon sun.

He picked up a ball and threw it for Joey a few times—surveying his environment. The yard, the netted frame, the makeshift pitcher's rubber, and the piece of plywood home plate.

He'd faced his fair share of challenges—no doubt about that—and he wasn't at all excited about starting high school, but he figured, whatever, three years and I'm done. Then I can forget the whole thing.

Little did he know, Brad would be inserting himself into the mix—making tenth grade something Will would always remember.

A Day At The Fair

There was the funky aroma of a rural lifestyle, the hum of heavy machinery, the wail of crying kids, and shrieks of panic—which meant only one thing: you were at the Mill Valley Fair.

The annual event drew kids from Mill Valley and its surrounding areas. And each and every one of them scraped together as many dollars as they could get their hands on, with the intent of blowing every penny. And for all its stereotypical trappings—4H Club entrants and all—what the Mill Valley Fair assured was a memory-making, summer-ending diversion—a week before all hell broke loose and school was back in session.

Mill Valley was at the tail end of an all-time-record-breaking heat wave. The fairgrounds were packed with a crowd happy to be outside, jamming as much as they could into summer's last few days.

For Mickey and Will, the joy of being fifteen years old with pockets full of cash could be bested by only one thing. And those boys were hypnotized by just that thing—there were girls. Lots of girls.

The crowds, zombie-like under the sensory overload coming at them from every direction, wandered with little intent.

Many would soon find out "those onions" were bait. They had been lured to the fair's most popular destination—one producing a savory fog permeating every corner of the landscape. There was just no smell like the smells coming from food trucks selling everything from the humble french fry to the bizarre confection—imagine portions of chocolate-covered cheesecake, battered and deep fried.

Any attempt to resist something double-dipped or married to slices of bacon would prove fruitless for most.

And there were rides—or rather, lineups with a few rides spaced in between. Here, screams of joy and terror topped the decibel chart.

This was also the spot where, every once in a while, someone would be separated from the what-in-the-hell-was-that they just ate.

Will and Mickey took a wide turn around a poor rider who'd just spent five minutes upside down, rotating in circles. The unfortunate kid was now bent over the remnants of a giant donut—which at one time had been stuffed with ice cream, fried chicken, and cream cheese jalapeños—now splayed on the ground in front of them.

The boys drifted aimlessly during their hour-and-a-half trek around the grounds. They hit the Zipper and the Drop Zone and pondered the Cliffhanger's thirty-minute lineup but quickly settled on a food-next itinerary.

After consulting the YOU ARE HERE map, they realized the most direct route to food-truck heaven was through the strip of pavement upon which every carnival expects to cash in.

If there was any chance you survived the gauntlet of deep-fried dining and stomach-churning rides, here you might at last be separated from what was left of your hard-earned cash—games of little to no chance.

A cross-section of fair attendees spent hours huddled together as spinning wheels drained dollars from their pockets.

"Either of you boys play baseball?" a carny called out from across the midway. "It's three balls for only half a buck, and you can win some really great prizes!"

Will and Mickey broke stride for a moment, considered the prospects, and were just about to get back on course.

"I'll make it four balls!" he called out, upping the ante.

Which was just enough to pique the boys' interest—so they took a little detour.

"Haven't had a winner all day!" the carny said.

He pegged Will as his primary target as the boys sauntered over to take a closer look.

"Y'all think you've got the stuff there, big man?" he mumbled around the unlit cigar clenched between his teeth.

Challenged, Will pulled a couple of quarters out of his pocket, and three balls were placed on the counter.

Will looked at the carny. "Probably won't need the fourth one anyway."

Fuzzy gopher targets sat on shelves adorned with crepe banners hanging decoratively across the front. Three tiers, the targets larger on the bottom and smaller on the top. If you knocked one off each tier, you got to pick your choice of any big prize.

The additional challenge was the HIT WOOD – NO GOOD sign—it had to be a clean hit with no bounces.

Will picked up a ball—he held it gently and rotated it slowly as he felt for the seams—then proceeded to nail a big gopher on the lower shelf.

The guy running the booth took note of Will's left hand—or rather, the lack thereof. He was also in some disbelief of the kid's throwing ability. He quickly stepped in front of Will.

"Slow down there, sharpshooter," he said before yelling out to the midway. "Take a look here, folks, we got a real pro!"

The short delay encouraged a few people strolling by to stop and watch.

Will picked up another ball and knocked a medium gopher off the second tier.

"I think I just got hustled," the carny mumbled to Will before calling out to the midway again. "C'mon folks, have a look at this kid! He's two for two!"

A handful more curious onlookers wandered over.

The carny stood between Will and the targets and started to put on a show. He juggled a few balls as he let the onlookers—prospective customers, optimistically speaking—know that Will was just one target away from winning a top prize.

Finally, he stepped aside, allowing Will to throw his third ball—but Will didn't rush. He took a minute to let the growing crowd behind him settle down.

They craned their necks.

Someone whispered, "Look, he only has one hand."

Will threw his third ball and caught just enough of a tiny little gopher on the top shelf that it spun around and toppled off the back, landing upright on the ground below.

"Winner, winner, chick'n dinner!" the carny shouted.

A kid in the crowd asked his mom if he could try.

"I'm in!" an older kid said to his friends.

Will was pointing to the stuffies hanging from the tent frame above. "I get to pick from any of those ones up there, right?"

"That's right, kid, pick any one you want," the carny said, glancing again at the stump of Will's left arm, "and promise me you won't come back. I don't wanna go broke!"

He winked at Will.

"With an arm like that, you're gonna be cashing some big cheques one day, my man."

The carny seemed to be speaking to the crowd watching Will as much as he was speaking to Will himself.

Will opted for an orange-and-black striped tiger—about the size of a medium dog.

"I'll see you in the show, kid!" the carny said as he flung the tiger to Will.

Then he tossed some balls to kids in the crowd. "Here's a few freebies. Now, who's next?"

Will and Mickey started walking down the midway with the sound of baseballs ricocheting off the shelves behind them.

Up ahead, Will saw Brad and his crew from school hanging around a midway game.

A Japanese family—a little girl and her parents—were holding hands as they walked toward Will and Mickey.

"Excuse me, sir, something for your daughter," Will said, tossing the tiger to the girl's dad as they passed.

The little girl shrieked, "For me?"

A couple of steps later, Will turned, looked behind him, then turned again.

"Hey Mick, did you see the girl in the purple hat? She must have been walking right behind us. Looks like she's with the family I gave the tiger to. She's a total ten!"

Keno, twenty-five-cent diggers, and a big red-and-black spinning wheel with crowns and anchors flanked them left and right.

"Girl? Where?" Mickey asked, his head swiveling from side to side.

"Never mind. Just keep walking, man, I need food!"

The girl—in the purple hat—shared a quick laugh with her family.

Then, shielding her eyes from the sun, she watched as Will and Mickey carried on up the midway.

That Girl

The boys stopped in front of a booth where a few people were busy trying to get a ring over the neck of a pop bottle lying on its side. As if that wasn't already hard enough, once they managed the feat, they had to stand the bottle up to win a prize—but nobody did.

"These games are rigged," Mickey said, just a bit too loud.

The guy operating the booth glared at Mickey, then lifted up a section of the counter and walked to the front of the booth. He nudged Mickey out of the way, picked up a stick, looped the ring around a pop bottle, and stood it up.

"Or there's a trick," he said, as he prompted Mickey to take the stick.

Mickey put his hands up in protest. "Right, or there's a trick."

Mickey looked back over his shoulder until he was sure they were out of earshot. "And if you don't know the trick, you might as well just hand the guy your cash and keep walking! And for the ones where there isn't a trick—yup, they're rigged.

"Seriously, Will, the tiger you won? That's a game of skill, especially since they've got a bunch of lead weights in the gopher's butt. It's a darn good thing you're a ringer, buddy!"

Will picked up the pace. "Yeah? Well, keep those dollars in your pocket, and let's get going. I'm starving, man. I need some vitamin D. It's time for dogs and drinks!"

"Hey, Lefty!"

Brad and his crew had been tossing nickels. You had to land one in the center circle to win five dollars, but again, no one did.

They stepped into the middle of the midway, blocking Will's and Mickey's path. Pretty much what Will expected.

"Nice hat," Brad said. "Thrift store?"

He removed his sunglasses and tucked one arm down the neck of his T-shirt.

Brad nailed it—Will's baseball cap was from a thrift store, and his logoed T-shirt was a knockoff.

"That's right," Will said. "If you want it, help yourself."

And just like that, Will had him. He'd challenged Brad to take his hat. He figured Brad didn't really want to try, but he also knew he couldn't resist. He wouldn't walk away. Not now. Not in front of his buddies.

Brad feinted a glance one way and then quickly stepped in to reach for Will's hat.

Before he got anywhere close, Will sidestepped and deflected Brad's reaching hand with his left forearm. When Brad tried to counter, Will reached up and snatched his sunglasses.

Tai sabaki.

Brad looked at the stump of Will's left arm and said, "Ugh, don't touch me with that thing."

"Tell you what, Brad," Will had backed off and was standing beside Mickey.

He looked at the sunglasses in his hand. "I could take everything you own—except for that one fact—you don't have anything I want.

"They're cheap, man—like you." He tossed the glasses to Brad.

Mickey and Will turned and walked away, but after a few steps, Mickey stopped. He glanced behind them.

"Hey, couple of things, Will. One, that guy is such a jerk, and two, can I join your karate club?"

Will laughed. "Geez, Mick, that'd be great. Karate would fit right in with your swimming—it's all core and hips, ya' know."

Will nudged Mickey on the shoulder. "And trust me, you would be adding to your room full of medals and trophies in no time—guaranteed!"

A few steps further down the midway, Mickey stopped again.

"Sup, Mick?"

"Hey, Will, you've stood up for me before—you remember, right?

"I hope you know, if I ever thought you couldn't handle Brad, or any of those guys—even two at a time—I'd step in. I'd be right beside you.

"It's just, if I'm in any kind of fight or whatever, no one is ever gonna take my side. I mean, I'm a Black kid, right?"

Will nodded, then he looked at Mickey and said, "Wait! You're Black?"

"Oh my god," Mickey shook his head and walked away. "I need some food."

They drifted over to a truck shaped like a giant dachshund.

As they stood checking out the Good Dawgz menu board, Will noticed the same family from before, a bit further up the midway. Now, there was a guy with them. They were in front of the Hole-in-One mini-donut stand—the little girl was holding the orange-and-black striped tiger.

"Hey, Mick, look—there she is again. The girl in the hat. That's the family I gave the tiger to. Wow, she is pretty—might be an eleven!"

It was a good long look for Will, then his stomach took over and he peeled his eyes away to check out the hot dog menu—Mickey continued looking up the midway—for good reason.

"Hey, Will," Mickey nudged him from behind, "don't look now, but that girl in the purple hat? She's walking this way."

"What?" Will's head spun around.

The girl was about halfway to where the boys were standing. Will glanced from side to side, trying to figure out why in the world she was coming toward them.

"Hi. My name's Hope. You gave my little sis the tiger?"

She glanced at Will's left arm.

Will was used to it—used to meeting people and having them notice he only had one hand. He didn't try to hide it. For him, it just *was*.

"Um, yeah. Oh, uh, my name is Will."

"Huh, same as my twin brother—William," Hope said. She glanced back at her family.

"That was really nice. Tigers are kind of a thing for us," she added.

Will glanced to where Hope's family was standing, then back at Hope.

"So, do you guys go to Valley View? I'm starting there next week. Tenth grade. I'm freaking out a little—don't know a soul. We just moved here a few weeks ago."

"Well, yeah, we do. I mean, we *will*," Mickey said. "We're going into tenth grade too."

"Sorry. This is my best friend, Mickey," Will said.

Hope nodded at Mickey. "Great! Well, when you see me looking lost in the hallways, help me out, OK?"

She took a look behind her.

"Guess I better get back to the fam. Looks like we're gettin' donuts!

"Anyway, thanks for the *tora,* Will.

"I mean tiger!

"I mean—oh my god," she laughed at herself and blushed—then spun around and skipped back toward her family, one hand holding her purple hat in place.

Will's eyes followed her every stride.

"Well, Mick, forget what I said about not wanting to head back to school next week!"

"That's what I like about you, Will—you're an optimist."

Mickey turned and ordered himself a foot-long.

THERE'S ALWAYS HOPE

Cap'n Hook

That summer of '99 was one for the books: a heatwave, Will's fifteenth birthday, the day at the fair, and high school right around the corner.

Will's mom was smart enough to wait until the fair left town, then she gifted Will a crisp fifty-dollar bill along with an autographed Tom Seaver baseball card in a rigid plastic sleeve.

"For your birthday from Big O. You and Mickey should hit the mall and pick up some threads for back-to-school."

They did, and on the way home, they dropped by Valley View High to check out the tenth grade homeroom student lists that were, as tradition dictated, taped to the windows of the school's main entrance. A mild curse confirmed Will and Mickey were on one list, and the only girl named Hope was on the other—with Brad.

Since their meeting at the fair, Will had fantasized all kinds of getting-to-know-Hope scenarios. After all, she was about the only girl who'd talked to him since his accident—that is, talked to him without continually glancing at his arm and getting some weird look on her face.

But learning Brad and Hope were in the same homeroom wasn't enough to kill the dream. Will figured he could still manufacture something, but he knew in his heart it was going to be a make-it-happen exercise.

When the big day arrived, Will decked himself out in a cool new plaid shirt paired with a denim jacket and took off. He met up with Mickey, and a short ride later, they parked their bikes and stepped into the very strange world called high school.

Will was split down the middle as he entered Valley View—he seemed to recall promising his mom he would "try hard,"—but pretty much everybody did that. And while he didn't want to disappoint her, trying *at all* hadn't been part of his repertoire for the last couple of years.

He was certain he was walking into three more years of hell—Brad et al. But there was a tinge of swagger in Will's step—he possessed a level of optimism and confidence he couldn't have predicted even a year earlier. Being asked to help out at the dojo, and his recent return to the baseball diamond, were a couple of giant strides.

That optimism was dealt its first blow when, on day one, he found, of all his courses, only English Composition 10 was shared with Hope. It was good news—English Comp was one of the core subjects that ran year-round, unlike the electives, which were split up by semester. That sliver of good news was tempered by the fact Brad was in the same class.

Will figured Brad was going to present the same challenges he had in middle school, and the first few days of high school proved him right—*Lefty* in the hallways. And as those first days rolled into weeks, Brad broadened his reach with a whole new crew of recruits.

Meanwhile, Hope was becoming one of the more popular girls.

For Will, Hope was most definitely the primary challenge, and Will calculated that integrating into her circle was going to take some strategic planning. To that end, he tried to position himself at opportune hallway locations, hoping for a not-so-completely chance meeting. It was a concrete plan that seldom worked.

Hope's schedule was complex.

She and her twin brother, William, usually got to school right at the morning bell—or later—and it seemed Hope rarely hung around after school. If she did, it was for track practice or a quick meeting with a teacher before she bolted out the door.

And Will had his own obligations. He joined the rugby and track teams, which put him on the field for after-school practices on Mondays and Wednesdays. Blitzing his paper route and heading to the dojo were priorities on Tuesdays and Thursdays.

It didn't take long for Will to realize getting on that girl's radar was going to require some guerrilla tactics.

One day, after the final bell, Mickey was in the hallway at the front office, scanning the trophy cases lining the wall. The boys usually met there and walked or rode home after school.

Will came up the stairs. "Hey, Mick."

"Hey, Will. How's the stalking going?"

"I don't know, Mick. I'd say she's avoiding me."

"You know what, Will? I don't think that's it. I think it's that she doesn't even know you exist."

"Ouch. Are you sure you're my best friend?" Will exaggerated an injury to his heart as they walked down the school's front steps. They unlocked their bikes and headed toward the street.

Brad was at the entrance, leaning against the fence with one of his buddies.

"Hey, Lefty, I didn't know you guys were still dating. It's really quite cute."

"Seriously, Brad? You are such a dickhead." Mickey glanced between Brad and his sidekick as he and Will passed by.

Before they were out of earshot, Brad fired another round. "Oh, and Lefty, stay away from Hope, would you? She told me that stump of yours creeps her out."

Will had seen Hope and Brad chumming it up in the hallways on more than one occasion. He knew they had a few classes together. A downer for sure, but Will recorded one small victory—he grabbed a seat one row away from Hope in English Comp.

And he randomly, and sometimes not so randomly, ran into her in the hall between classes. In fact, he created a bit of a scoring system, grading every *Hi. How's things going?* hallway interaction on a scale of one to ten.

"You are aware that's a bit creepy, right, Will?" Mickey said after Will announced a recent seven out of ten.

***

October 31 rolled around, and the Halloween dance was the place to be.

The gym was packed with mad scientists carrying beakers of slimy green eyeballs, ex-presidents, and every famous or infamous celebrity one could imagine.

The event was in full swing, and Mickey, clad in a nondescript trench coat, and Will were standing by the snacks table.

Hope and a couple of friends snuck up behind them.

"Hi, Mick. And you are?" Hope asked.

"How should I put this?" Mickey said. "I'm actually a bit less of a 'Who am I?' and more of a 'What am I?' Now excuse me, ladies."

Mickey stepped between Hope and her friends, took a dozen steps—gracefully spun around—and strode back toward the table.

It took a moment for his onlookers to realize—one of the arms of Mickey's trench coat was stuffed with newspaper and tucked in the coat's pocket—while inside the trench coat, Mickey held the handle of a papier-mâché leg. The fake leg was clad in a pant leg and shoe that mirrored the pants and shoes on his real legs.

With each stride, he pulled off the gait of a three-legged man.

Hope erupted with laughter. "That is unbelievable! And honestly, Mick, it's a little bit twisted!"

"Well, thank you!" Mickey said. "And I'm guessing you're an angel?"

"Every year since I was six!" Hope replied.

"And which pirate are you?" one of Hope's friends asked Will.

"Arrgh, Cap'n Hook," Will replied. "Kind of my go-to."

He held up his left arm, adorned with a cardboard and tinfoil hook he'd fashioned with his mom's help.

"Perfect," said Hope, as she grabbed a couple of carrot sticks. "I'll bring my angel streak to an end and be Tinker Bell instead. Maybe we can win a prize."

The girls waved to an incoming group of scantily clad nurses, then pushed their way into the chaotic crowd.

Hope turned and said, "Hey, Will, we're going to hang out in the bleachers for a while, but let's dance later, OK?"

"Oh, I'll be dancing, all right!" Mickey yelled after them. "You know I'll be dancing!"

"Holy crap, Mick! What just happened?"

"I take it all back, man. She *does* know you exist. And lucky you—she's got a thing for pirates."

Order Your Pizza

Will accepted the life-altering reality of his accident—how could he not? But he and his mom could still find things to be thankful for. The costs of therapy and his prosthetic were covered, and they now owned their house outright, thanks to his dad's life insurance policy—which relieved a lot, but not all, of the financial pressures.

Because of Will's age, it was decided his first prosthetic would be a basic body-powered hand prosthesis. As you can imagine, Will wasn't thrilled with the look of the thing—a mechanical device with a pulley system that activated its pinchers.

Around the house, Will and his mom talked about putting every extra dollar toward a bionic hand—a myoelectric hand prosthesis. They both knew it was a long-term plan—leading-edge technologies could run well over fifty thousand dollars—but at least it was a plan.

Post-amputation therapy for Will included both physical and emotional recovery plans. Both were an eye-opening immersion into the world of amputations. Will often met people who were not nearly as fortunate as he was, and as time passed, his perspectives changed.

Will learned that only a generation earlier, less than half of upper-body amputees even bothered with a prosthetic—they just tried to hide their disability. Will was continually reminded how important it was to be proficient with a prosthetic, learning it would become a huge factor in his long-term quality of life. But as important as that was, he was also taught to be comfortable being himself—his new normal.

It didn't happen on day one, but over time, he got the message.

One day Will was rushing out the door to some school event. His mom commented, "You're going commando?"

Will's answer filled her with pride—"Yup, I say screw 'em—if they mind, they don't matter."

She knew her son was known as the one-handed kid, but she also knew he was determined not to let it define him.

***

A month after the Halloween dance, Big O was brought over to the house for Thanksgiving dinner. He and Will ate almost two whole pies, which turned out to be an inspiration for Will.

November was torn off the calendar, and in early December, a decorated Christmas tree popped up in the school's foyer. A poster on the wall advertised that the annual Christmas Fair was scheduled for the last Saturday before the winter break. Those wanting to book a table could apply at the office.

Mickey and Will persuaded the food services teacher to give them access to the ovens in the food lab.

The next day, they approached the owner of Mill Valley's premier restaurant supply company. He succumbed to their hard sell, declared it a worthy cause, and sold them products at cost. As he ushered the boys out of his office, he mumbled something about needing guys like them on his sales team.

On the day of the Christmas Fair, at 10:00 in the morning, Mickey's dad dropped Will, Mickey, and their fifty frozen pies off at school.

The boys fired up the ovens and baked a dozen pies while they set up their booth. When the doors opened at 1:00 in the afternoon, sales took off. Every time a couple of pies came out of an oven, two more went in.

The boys took turns—one running the booth, the other shuttling slices of pie from the kitchen, across the hall, and into the gym.

"Coming through!" Will hollered as he swept in with a tray held over his head.

He dropped the load—two slices of apple and two slices of cherry—on the table and pivoted back to the cafeteria. Mickey smothered a slice with whipped cream and sent a happy customer on their way.

It was about 2:30 in the afternoon when Hope and William happened by, just as Will carried in a tray with four more slices.

"Guys? I am impressed!" Hope said as she dropped some bills in the collection jar.

"William will take an apple," Hope said—William nodded—"and I'll have one of those cherry. And Mick, you, my friend, can go heavy with the whipped cream on both of them."

Hope glanced around at some of the other vendors. "This is such a great idea. Seriously, you are by far the busiest booth here!"

They chatted for a couple of minutes, then Hope and William sauntered off to shop tables piled high with Christmas crafts.

"Too bad they left—I was just about to do a math joke about pi," Will said.

"Huh?" Mickey put a hand to his forehead. "Dude, you're making progress. Don't blow it!"

A couple of days later, everyone was back at school and in good spirits—the final week before the Christmas break can do that.

Some guys standing in the foyer near the trophy cases called Will over.

"Double Dub, sup?"

A few of Will's rugby teammates joined the group. They stood checking out a poster promoting the upcoming annual rugby tournament.

Just then Brad and crew walked through the school's front door.

Will took notice.

Brad. Could a person be any more wrapped up in their own bravado?

It was obvious he came from money—he dressed like a somebody and had the enviable good looks and swagger that left no doubt—he thought he was.

And he got the girls—so, yup, Will was jealous.

By this point in the year, Brad had become the default leader of a growing group calling Will *Lefty*—presenting an ever-greater challenge for Will to overcome.

"I'm telling ya', gentlemen, it was nothing but mountains and valleys for me yesterday," Brad bragged to his audience, explaining Hope was his geography partner and they'd been working on an assignment together.

"Oh yeah, that Hope is a fine collection of mountains and valleys!"

It was painfully obvious Brad detailed this bit of news at an amplified volume, knowing Will was within earshot.

Are you kidding me? Will thought as he strolled down the hall to his philosophy class. *Anyone but Brad. Please. Anyone.*

A few days later, Valley View closed for the break.

On the following Saturday, Mickey and Will were walking around the downtown streets.

"You should have heard him in the hallway, Mick. I wanted to puke!"

"It's OK, man. Every time she spends ten minutes with the guy, she's gonna find out everything she needs to know. And that, my friend, is gonna help you get your pizza."

Will pondered Mickey's sage advice for about half a second, then asked the obvious question. "What in the heck are you talking about?"

Mickey stopped Will in his tracks.

"Look. Here's what my dad says.

"The other day, we were watching a movie, and he says, 'So, Mick, any big hopes and dreams for the new year?' and I said, 'Yup, of course!'

"Then he said, 'Well, did you make the call?' and I said, 'What do you mean?'

"And he says, 'Mick, suppose I asked if you wanted a slice of pizza. You'd say sure, right?' and I was like, 'Duh!'

"And he said, 'Humor me. Go open the front door.'

"So I did, and he asks, 'Is there a guy there with a pizza?'

"Well, I looked at him like he was nuts and said, 'No.'

"Then he says, 'Well, Mick, you gotta understand somethin'. The universe works the same way as pizza delivery. If you want it, you gotta order it up, and you gotta tell the universe exactly what you want.

"If you don't do that, ain't no pizza gonna be comin' to your front door.'"

Mickey was done with his rambling life lesson, and Will took a moment to digest things.

"Hmm," he said. "OK then, universe. I'm placing my order!"

"Perfect. Now it's just a matter of time!" Mickey said as they made a hard left into a sports memorabilia store.

That night, Will took it one step further.

After dinner he was sitting in his room reading. He'd retrieved the book his mom suggested way back when, the one with all the math and baseball stuff.

I'm gonna write them all down so I can remember what I ordered, he thought.

He grabbed a sheet of paper and drafted a list:

1. I'm going to go on a date with Hope.
2. I'm going to get my *shodan*.
3. I'm going to make the all-star team ~~this~~ next season.

Crossing out the word *this* and writing *next*, confirmed he was both an optimist and a realist.

He folded the piece of paper, put it with his collectibles, and tucked the box into his desk drawer.

It's Just Wrong

January 1 arrived, bringing with it a brand new century—the world hadn't imploded, so it was business as usual.

While the whole January-back-to-school thing had all the attributes of a trip to the dentist, what would soon become clear was that the universe had been listening to Will, and things were about to take a decidedly positive turn.

During the first week of the new semester, classes were in full swing. Will was sitting alone at a two-seat table in the back of the room, waiting for his Entrepreneurial Studies class to start.

He was gazing out the window—daydreaming. It was that time of year—the world outside looked like a black-and-white photo, and things in Will's head shared roughly the same palette.

Suddenly, out of the corner of his eye, he saw Hope walk through the classroom door.

Thoughts in his mind developed in quick succession. *What is she doing here?* And more importantly, *What in the heck is it about her that makes my stomach do what it just did?*

Hope scanned the room, then hurried to the empty spot beside Will and plunked her stuff on the table.

"Just switched out of my Fashion Design class so I can get a head start on being a billionaire," she said as she sat down. "I'm thinking pies. And by the way, Will, nice job at the Christmas Fair."

Later that day, Mickey and Will met in the hall near the office.

"OK. Dreams come true, Mick. Hope is now in my Entrepreneurial Studies class. She walked in and sat down right beside me today!"

"Well, you placed the order," Mickey replied.

A few days later, the boys were cruising home on their bikes. Will explained the situation.

"I'm telling ya', Mick, I don't think the girl ever stands still. We've had a few chats, right? Turns out she takes piano, she's smart, she does some kind of martial art, and she sings."

"OK, well, what'd ya' think she was—a bag of rocks?" Mickey replied.

"And listen, Will, it's like I said—you're making progress. Ya' just gotta give it a bit of time."

"I mean, seriously, how can she not fall for a guy with one hand and two big scars on his face?"

Will considered things for a second.

"Thanks, Mick. You're a huge help."

"But you know what, I think maybe you're right. I *am* making some progress, and even though when I see her in the hall she's talking to Brad or one of those other jerks, eventually, she is going to find me irresistible."

"Well, dude, as they say—you'll know when you know."

Truer words were never spoken, and about a month later, on a Saturday afternoon, Will was provided with more information.

Mickey and Will were on the Valley View rugby field.

The three local high schools were engaged in the sixth annual tenth-grade boys' rugby tournament. Mill Valley bragging rights were on the line.

The games were quick and painful—seven players per side with a fifteen-minute game clock. Each team played four games in the double round-robin, and the trophy went to the team with the highest net points.

This year's tournament was heavily advertised at school. Posters in the hallways detailed the matchups in the round robin and reflected a competitive tone by showing previous years' trophy winners and their win, loss, and net points records.

One poster in particular had people chuckling. A student from the Art Department drew a great cartoon of two rugby players clashing head-to-head—the caption read, *You'll Need Leather Balls for This Tournament.*

Along with the Valley View supporters, a huge contingent of fans from Mill Valley's other high schools—River Heights and South Bend—were there to watch.

It was a perfect day for a rugby tournament—brutally cold and pouring rain. The concession was cranking out hot drinks to spectators huddled under blankets in the bleachers or lining the sides of the pitch—their every breath coming out in white clouds.

By the time the afternoon matches got underway, the field was a muddy quagmire.

Will's team won and lost close matches in the morning but easily outscored their opponent in the first of the afternoon games. That victory gave them a net points tally, putting them in contention for the trophy.

Twelve minutes into their final game, the players were standing around, waiting for things to resume—a trainer was attending to an injured ankle.

Jerseys and shorts were caked with mud. Blood trickled from torn knees and elbows.

Mickey gave Will a tap on the shoulder. "Don't look."

"I know," Will said as he snuck another quick glance toward the sidelines.

Hope was standing under an umbrella with Brad.

"Duckwater," Will muttered quietly.

Immediately after play restarted, Will had the ball tucked under his arm and was speeding down the field. He outmaneuvered two would-be tacklers and straight-armed another out of the way before his shirt was grabbed from behind. He almost broke free, but another player caught him around the waist. Will kept pumping forward as he spun off balance—just before going down, he managed to lateral a pass. His teammate carried the ball the final fifteen yards for the try. Valley View kicked the conversion and took the lead.

Valley View fans clapped and cheered as the players headed back to midfield for the kick restart.

Brad called out from the sidelines, "Nice play, Lefty!" as Will jogged by.

Will was bent over with his hand on his knee, catching his breath. Steam rose from his back. He wiped the mud from his brow with the stump of his arm, his face beet red—less from exertion than from Brad's comment—and his company.

Mickey gave him a pat on the back. "Great effort, Will."

The game ended, the tournament ended, and the players were in the change room, chugging sodas and scarfing bags of chips the coach plopped down on the dressing-room table.

What Will hadn't seen after his "great effort," and Brad's comment, was Hope letting Brad know the *Lefty* thing wasn't cool.

"Seriously, Brad? You say something like that out loud and expect to get away with it? Will is a nice guy. He has a disability, but he's out there giving his best effort."

"It was a joke—lighten up," Brad scoffed.

"No! I won't lighten up. It's not funny, and it's just wrong." Hope replied.

A moment later, Hope left the shelter of Brad's umbrella to sit with more palatable friends in the bleachers. That was the last time Brad and Hope were ever to be found in close proximity. And things were about to get worse for Brad.

Later, showered and changed, and with backpacks full of wet and stinking rugby gear, the boys started the walk home.

Though it hardly seemed possible, the temperature dropped another couple of degrees, and a cruel mix of rain and snow began to fall.

"So fun!" Mickey said as they walked along, munching on bags of chips they'd grabbed for the road. "Could you believe the size of that kid from River Heights? Pretty sure the guy had a mustache!"

"No kidding. I thought he was the bus driver," Will laughed.

They'd only gone a couple of blocks when Hope caught up to them.

"Can I walk with you guys?" she asked.

"Sure," Mickey answered. He glanced at Will.

Will raised his eyebrows in an *I have no idea* kind of way.

Understood

A month later, the universe answered Will's call again—though this response could have made him second-guess his order.

It was Wednesday morning. The recess bell rang, and the hall was quickly packed with kids leaving their first class of the day.

Will's head was buried in his locker. He'd started the day with History and was looking forward to his next class, Phys Ed. As usual, Mickey would drop by his locker—they'd grab something quick from the cafeteria, then head to the gym.

Seeing Hope's brother, William, walk by on his way to the cafeteria, Will thought maybe Hope would be coming down this way. Her locker was up a short flight of stairs and down the hall, about three or four classrooms past the office.

Hope and her brother often met up at recess and lunch, so Will was taking his time puttering around—periodically glancing up the hall toward the office. The Hope watch. Stalking 101.

Mickey came along. "How long are you going to pretend you can't find your lunch?"

"Yeah, yeah," Will said, giving up and slamming the locker door.

Will and Mickey headed down the short corridor into the cafeteria just as William was walking out with a tray of cheesy nachos and a large fountain drink.

"William," Will nodded.

"Will," William nodded back.

A few seconds later, there was a *splosh* sound, followed by someone shouting, "What the hell!"

Will and Mickey turned and walked toward the commotion.

Brad was standing in a puddle of orange soda—a cup and its contents lay on the floor, the lid and straw a few inches away. Nachos had gone flying everywhere, except for the half dozen stuck, along with their cheesy topping, to Brad's letterman jacket. A healthy portion of

William's drink was all over Brad's crotch and had run down his pant legs. Even his white running shoes were stained orange.

"Nice one, you moron!" Brad yelled. He shoved William—William stumbled and fell.

Will rushed in, shouting, "Brad, what are you doing?" He pushed Brad back. "Leave him alone."

Brad stepped forward, grabbed Will, spun him around, and shoved him hard against the opposite wall.

"Back off, Lefty! Someone's gettin' their ass kicked!"

Then he turned toward William, who was just getting to his feet with Mickey's help.

Hope, coming down the stairs from the office, saw and heard the exchange between Will and Brad.

As Brad moved toward her brother, screaming, "You're a freakin' retard!" Hope stepped in between them.

She grabbed Brad's right arm with her left hand and threw her right arm across his chest. Simultaneously, she placed her right leg behind Brad's right leg. Then she started to turn, drawing her left leg back— she was like the center of a clock, sweeping counterclockwise.

It was a lightning-quick move.

Hope kept turning, and in just a moment, Brad was off balance. She lowered him gently into the orange soda puddle on the floor.

Hope positioned herself so she had Brad's right hand secured in a wrist lock. Then she levered him over, forcing him to support himself on his other elbow.

Brad tried to get up, but she twisted his wrist, and he plopped back down into the puddle, wincing.

"Brad, I'm pretty sure you just used the word..." Hope's voice trailed off. "Actually, I'm not even going to repeat it."

She applied a bit more pressure to Brad's wrist.

"I'm sorry," Brad said quietly.

Hope didn't raise her voice. She spoke in an even, measured tone— only a few people in the gathered crowd even heard her speak.

"Well, Brad, all I can say is don't use that word, and don't ever think of laying a hand on my brother."

Mr. Phelps, the biology teacher, came around the corner, saw the crowd, and asked if everything was OK.

Brad was wrestling himself to his feet, glowering at Hope.

William told the teacher he was fine, then turned to Brad, saying, "Sorry about that, Brad, but you came running around the corner real fast, and I didn't have time to get out of the way."

Hope put a finger in Brad's face. "Ever. Understood?"

The Will-and-Brad mix-up was another one of those moments—one of those times in Will's life when he stepped off the sideline and got involved. He knew he'd done the right thing but suspected Brad might not see it that way. True enough, it wasn't over.

Once things were broken up, Will and Mickey rushed to the gym.

"Well, that was pretty intense!" Mickey said as they jogged down the hallway.

"That guy is such a wing nut," Will shook his head. "Can't imagine what he was thinking, shoving William like that—I mean, come on!"

They quickly changed into their Phys Ed gear, stashed their clothes in lockers, and headed out to the track where the rest of the class was warming up.

They ran in the middle of the pack for the one-mile run. Then, with that out of the way, the highlight of the class: floor hockey. Will defaulted to goalie and managed to pick up "the wall" as a nickname.

After class, most of the guys grabbed a quick shower.

Will stood in front of the mirror, putting on deodorant and checking his hair.

"Hey, dude, it's English Comp, not the prom!"

Will laughed. "You mean I rented a limo for nothing?

"Hey, what are you doing for your spare, Mick?"

"I'm done for the day, my friend. Private lesson this afternoon—stroke improvement. Big meet in a couple of weeks. My dad's picking me up, we're grabbing lunch, then off to the pool."

"What? Wednesday afternoon off? Jealous!" Will held out a fist.

"And you've got English Comp—say hi to Brad for me!" Mickey bumped Will's offering and was out the door.

A minute or so later, Will was on the way to class. His desk, halfway down the row running along the wall of windows, sat empty.

Hope was at her desk, one row over and one desk ahead of Will's.

Brad was standing beside his desk—the second seat in the first row near the classroom entrance. His pants still bore the remnants of William's drink, making it look like he'd pissed himself—and he was fuming.

If I Were You

Will hurried down the hall, figuring he'd make it to class just as the final bell rang. He passed the office, saw Mr. Paulson, the English Comp teacher, speaking with the principal, and throttled back his pace a bit.

As he walked into the classroom, Brad took a couple of steps toward the front. He stood blocking Will's access. It was clear he wanted to put on a show.

"Hey, buddy, if I were you, I'd keep my nose out of other people's business. Got it?" Brad barked, arms crossed. "'Cause next time, I will gladly kick your ass for you."

The classroom went still. By now, almost everyone knew about the morning's shoving match. The gossip included how Hope had taken Brad for a little dance before sitting him in a puddle on the floor—and that Brad was choked.

Thirty-two kids. Dead silence. Most of them wondering, *Is this happening now?*

"Really, Brad? Well, you are definitely welcome to try, I guess."

Will's response was like a Laurel and Hardy routine. With every *you* and *me*, his head nodded from one side to the other.

"But if I were you, I wouldn't tell me what you would do if you were me—because all I'd have to do is tell Hope on ya', and then she'd drop you on your ass again!

"Oh, and did you wet yourself?"

He sidestepped Brad, bumping his shoulder as he passed by.

Brad contemplated retaliating just as Mr. Paulson entered the room.

"Later, buddy. Later," he muttered, watching as Will walked away.

Will hustled toward his desk, diverting so he could pass by Hope, where he found her hand extended for a low five.

The class buzzed.

Whispers in the hallways for the rest of the day were all about the morning drama.

Later in the afternoon, well after the final bell, Will was standing at his locker. He wasn't in a rush. There was no track practice this early in the year, and being a Wednesday, he didn't have to deliver papers or head to the dojo.

The hallways had mostly cleared out. A couple of straggling students were at a locker at the bottom of the stairs—a bit up the hall and across from Will. It was a girl from English Comp and her friend.

Brad had sat on the embarrassment of being taken down by Hope all morning. That embarrassment blossomed into anger in the English Comp classroom, and now that he could see his target in front of him, it morphed into full-on rage.

With no hesitation in his step, Brad stormed past the office, charged down the stairs, past the two girls, and made a beeline toward Will.

Will didn't see Brad coming until he was almost on top of him.

"You're done, buddy!" Brad screamed.

He grabbed Will by the front of his shirt. Fabric tore, and buttons popped—pinging off the linoleum floor. He pushed him hard against the bank of lockers.

"Calm down, asshole!" Will shouted.

Will pushed back and broke free, giving himself a bit of space—but Brad came in throwing punches up around the head. Very quickly, Will's nose was gushing.

Brad's size gave him a tremendous advantage.

Will's prosthetic—torn loose—was more of a liability than anything else. All he could do was block. He ducked and spun away, looking for an opening to strike. At one point, he landed a solid blow, catching Brad on the jaw, but clearly, it wasn't going to be enough.

Brad finally got a grip on what was left of Will's shirt and spun him hard into the lockers on the other side of the hall. He followed up with another hail of punches to Will's ribs.

This was serious.

By now, one of the girls had run up the stairs to the office and was leading the vice-principal—a big guy with a healthy beard and aging tattoos—back toward the ruckus.

Will spun and sidestepped, attempting to get some position. He swung hard with his left forearm and caught Brad on the side of the head, then stepped in and landed another right. It slowed Brad down for just a second.

But Brad came in with his fists again. Will did his best to defend and strike, but Brad had the upper hand. He managed to get Will in a headlock and landed convincing blows as the teacher ran toward them.

"Hey, hey—break it up!" the teacher bellowed, separating the two combatants. He grabbed them by their collars. "Both of you! Up the stairs to the office. Now!"

Will sat on a chair, a wad of tissue held against his bloodied nose, a black eye starting to form. Brad was in a private office with the principal. The girl who witnessed the onset of the fight was in another office, telling the vice-principal her version of events.

After five or ten minutes, Brad emerged and was escorted out of the principal's office. One final threat towards Will, "Hey, Lefty, I won't be seeing you around town, but if you do ever cross my path again, just remember, this isn't over."

Will was next to be interviewed. His mom had been called and was on the way.

***

Brad wasn't back at school the following morning. Rumors swirled around the hallways.

One of Brad's buddies said he wouldn't be coming back at all. They said Brad's whole family was moving to a big city hundreds of miles away. They said it had been in the works for a couple of months— something about a job.

"Honestly, the guy was just a mosquito to me. An annoyance. 'Duckwater,' as Big O calls it." Will and Mickey were walking to class.

Mickey side-eyed him. "That's twice with the duck water? Dare I ask?"

"You know, the water that runs off a duck's back."

"Oh my god, never shoulda opened my mouth."

***

Hope caught up with Will in the hallway.

"Yikes, Will, that's quite a shiner you've got there. Are you OK?"

Will shuffled his feet. "Yeah, yeah, I'm fine. Only hurts when I laugh," he chuckled.

"Hey, seriously though, Will, thanks for helping William yesterday." Hope tilted her head as she surveyed the damage to Will's face.

Will shrugged. "I don't know why Brad flipped out like that. It was no big deal—just an accident. I mean, he probably caused the whole thing anyway. I hope William wasn't too upset."

"Yeah, actually, he was kind of freaked out," Hope replied.

Will nodded. "Me too, to be honest.

"I was pretty happy you came along when you did—kinda saved my butt, Hope!

"Mind you, I could have used your help when he was trying to finish me off after school!"

They both laughed.

"I'll be sure not to do anything to make you mad at me—where did you learn that wrist thing anyway?" Will asked.

Hope just smiled.

You Didn't Tell Me That

During the weeks after Brad left Valley View, Hope and Will became more friendly. They had a few more interactions in the hallways and chatted in class, but it seemed to Will she was always giving him an *I'm-too-busy* vibe.

Will thought he'd made some progress at the Halloween dance—but that was months ago. And he knew she'd been impressed with the Christmas pie table. The walk home after the rugby tournament was something, not to mention the whole Brad thing.

But as Will explained, "I don't know, Mick. One day we seem all buddy-buddy, and the next day, it's business only."

One afternoon, Hope caught Will off guard. She was waiting for him after his history lesson.

"Hey, Will, you're going to be at the River Heights long-weekend track meet, right?"

"Oh yeah. Anything to skip out on a Friday afternoon."

Hope smiled. "How are things going for you out there? You do hurdles and high jump?"

They started walking down the hall.

"Um, it's OK. I mean, I love the hurdles, but high jump and steeplechase are pretty hit-and-miss. Mostly miss."

"Oops, this is me," Hope said, ducking into a classroom.

Will shrugged and carried on down the hall.

***

Will powered out of the blocks, arms pumping and legs pounding down the track. At the tape, he knew he was in the top three.

He and two other runners were corralled toward the podium, where Will received the silver medal in the 10-by-110 hurdles. Later in the meet, he finished just out of the medals in the 1,000-meter steeplechase and fouled out early in the high jump.

Hope won four gold medals—high jump, 100-meter, 200-meter, and as the anchor in the 400-meter relay.

On Saturday afternoon, just before the meet wrapped up, everyone on the track team got together for a group photo. Will suspected the picture would be in the school yearbook. He reminded himself to take twenty bucks from his paper route money and put in an order.

The May track meet signaled the school year's final hump. Summer was in sight. Prepping for exams would start soon, the talent show was in mid-June, and if you didn't screw up your finals, the last couple of weeks of class were basically a party.

Even though year one of high school had started lukewarm for Will, by the time June rolled around, he was feeling at the top of his game. He was a fixture at the dojo and would be testing for his brown belt in a couple of weeks. And he was having a nice season of baseball—thanks to the amount of time Raj spent with him.

He even gained some attention as a one-handed baseball player.

***

The lunch hour was about half over, and Hope was sitting alone in the cafeteria when Will walked in. He'd planned on grabbing a bag of chips and heading to the library, but he saw Hope sitting there and thought, *What the heck—take a chance.*

She had her nose stuck in a physics textbook and was nibbling on some seaweed papers. Will approached the other side of the table. "OK if I join you?"

She looked up. "Hmm, Mr. Williams. Please do.

"So, Will, a couple of the girls in my chem class were talking about you this morning," Hope said as Will slid onto the seat across from her.

"Talking about me?" Will asked.

"They said you're some kind of hotshot baseball player. They saw your picture in the paper and said you were on the news."

Will raised his eyebrows and chuckled as his face turned beet red. "Well, um—"

Hope interrupted, "You didn't tell me that, Will."

Will looked at Hope over the top of her physics text. "Well, yeah, I'm back playing baseball again, and it's actually goin' OK."

Will had made it into the sports section of the local paper, where they printed a picture of him taking a throw at first base—stretching out with his right hand, his arm stump flared out to the side. There was another picture with him at the plate, batting one-handed. And he was on the local TV news one Saturday evening after a camera crew showed up at Allenby and filmed him pitching.

"Interesting," Hope said.

"I couldn't play at all after my accident, right?" Will nodded at his prosthetic. "I missed two full seasons. I was doing rehab the first year, and the next year, I was still getting used to things. My doctors didn't think it was a good idea to push it.

"But Mickey and I practice a lot, and now I'm back at it for real. Having fun! This is my second season playing, actually."

"Huh. That's great." Hope laid her book on the table.

"Yeah, my first year back was—well, let's say it was pretty interesting!" Will realized how quickly he was talking and did his best to pump the brakes. "I spent a lot of time in right field, but my coach also put me at first a few times, and I didn't totally suck, which was something. And he let me pitch quite a bit, which was really cool."

Will paused for a second. "This year, it's a lot different, though. I don't know why, but I seem to be really getting the hang of it—pitching, I mean."

"Do you bat?" Hope asked.

"Yeah, yeah, I bunt a lot. But if they creep in, I make 'em pay! I actually got an inside-the-park home run a few games ago. Though, full disclosure, I think they made three errors on the play!

"But what's really interesting is, Raj—my coach. This is the second year in a row he's drafted Mickey and me. Not sure why he does it, but super happy he does! Like I said, he's teaching me how to think like a pitcher. And I'm beginning to believe all the time I waste out in my backyard is paying off. Don't tell my math teacher."

Hope laughed. "Oh, I hear ya'. I've got her too—Ms. Brumweid, the teacher that fun forgot!

"But that's kind of amazing, you know. I mean, you're taking karate too, right? Playing baseball and rugby? And you're on the track team?

"You know, Will, I'm actually starting to wonder if you're secretly Superman."

Will just laughed and thought, *How does she know I'm taking karate?*

"Yeah, well, not many people know this, but there have been three one-handed baseball players in the majors. One of them even threw a no-hitter for the Yankees!"

"Really?" Hope said. "So how do you do it? Catch and throw, I mean?"

Will explained the gyrations he'd mastered.

"Seriously? When is your next game? I'll come out and watch."

Mickey is not going to believe this, Will thought.

"Um, well, we're away this weekend, but we've got a few home games left. Next Thursday, we play at Allenby. Playoffs are at the end of June, then things wrap up. They have an all-star team, but I doubt I'm making it this year."

"Anything else going on this summer?" Hope asked, reaching across the table and helping herself to one of Will's chips.

"A couple of weeks at Mickey's family cabin on the lake. We're going whitewater rafting too." Will replied. "And before you even ask, I'm gonna tape my left arm to the paddle."

Hope chuckled. "You're funny."

"And water skiing—there's a challenge. Mosquitoes—another challenge! Which takes us to the last couple of weeks of summer. The fair comes to town, then it's eleventh grade!"

"Nice," Hope said, checking the time. "Hey, I have to run. Physics! See ya' later, OK?"

The following Thursday, Hope came to Will's baseball game. Will spotted her in the stands. He ran the stump of his arm over the initials on his glove.

She hung around after the game.

After Raj's post-game talk, Will and Mickey emerged from the dugout, and the three of them sat in the bleachers, finishing off a couple of candy bags as they tossed a ball for Joey.

The next day at school, after the final bell rang, Will walked past the office, down the stairs, and found Hope leaning against his locker.

"Hi, Will."

"Hey, Hope. What's up?"

"Um, my family and I are heading back to Japan for our summer visit. Leaving this weekend, actually. And I probably won't be back until at least the middle of September. Might even be later."

"Wow, that sounds amazing. Have a great trip."

"Yeah, though I'll be in full catch-up mode when I get back. But you'll be here, right?"

Four months passed, and Hope was nowhere to be seen.

Know Hope

The wind howled, and the rain came down sideways. The local paper dubbed it *"Aug-uary,"* though Will and Mickey still managed to shake the dust off their wallets as they splashed around the fairgrounds.

A few days before school started, the boys rode over to Valley View—this time to check the eleventh grade homeroom assignments. Will stood silently, looking at the rosters. Hope's name was once again assigned to the other homeroom.

A week later, the doors at Valley View were flung open, and the packed hallways teemed with the high-energy buzz of back-to-school.

In English Comp 11, Mr. Paulson called the roll at the beginning of the first class.

"Hope Nakano?"

No answer.

Hmm, Will thought. *We're in the same class. That's a win.*

The same thing happened in Advanced Math.

September became October. The Halloween dance came and went.

A week into November, Will was losing faith. Hope was supposed to be in two of his classes—her name was on the lists—but she never showed up.

Will figured maybe her family had moved away permanently. He knew Hope's dad had a high-profile job in the lumber industry—that was the reason they moved to Mill Valley in the first place. His business with Japan meant he traveled back and forth a lot. Will wondered if maybe he'd been relocated to a new office.

Then one day, a Thursday, Will spotted Hope ducking out the doors leading to the portable classrooms set up to handle the overflow of kids enrolled this year.

Then nothing. Not in class, not in the hallways, not in the cafeteria.

Girl's a ghost, Will thought.

The following Tuesday at lunchtime, Will was in the cafeteria—and suddenly, there she was, standing on the other side of the table with a tray in her hands.

"Oh, I'm glad I found you. I'm way behind in math—so lucky you're in my class. Can you help me?" she asked, placing her tray on the table and sitting down.

Hope and Will ate and talked through the lunch hour.

The next day, Hope and William met up with Will and Mickey in the cafeteria again.

When the lunch hour ended, William and Mickey packed up and headed for class—Hope and Will stayed behind. It turned out they had the same spare—Wednesdays, right after lunch.

Conversation quickly turned to Hope's trip to Japan, and she filled Will in on the summer she'd spent in the sweltering heat of Osaka.

"You would not believe it! Ninety percent humidity, hot, hot, hot, and everybody is sweating! Our everyday routine was: wake up and head to the mall. It was about the only place to find some relief. Though, I have to tell you, a mall in Japan is an absolute cultural experience compared to what's going on in Mill Valley—especially if you like Godzilla."

Over the next few Wednesday spares, Will and Hope hanging out in the cafeteria became a regular thing.

Hope told Will a little about her family back in Japan, blending in some family history—including the fact her grandfather had been a very successful baseball player. She wondered if Will knew about Japanese baseball.

Will had been paying attention, of course, but this was important new information, and he immediately started grilling Hope on exactly what "successful" meant.

She was a bit evasive but confessed her grandfather got some added perks when they went to games, and she'd probably watched ten over the summer.

Eventually, she explained to Will that her grandfather—her mom's dad—had gone to university and then played for the Hanshin Tigers in Osaka. He had a string of good seasons, and after he retired, he lined up a job in the North American minor leagues as a pitching coach. Then he and her grandmother made the move.

"They had a great life here, but they moved back to Japan shortly after my mom and dad met. My mom wasn't going anywhere once she met my dad—love at first sight, she likes to tell me. So here we are, living happily ever after.

"That's why I go back to Japan every summer. My mom gets to see her mom and dad, and I get spoiled by my grandparents."

Will was fascinated. He wanted to know all about Hope's grandfather. The conversation often veered off in other directions, but it usually circled back around to the Tigers.

A couple of Wednesdays later, sitting in the cafeteria, Hope and Will were thumbing through a stack of pictures from Hope's trip to Japan. Will was captivated by stories of Japanese culture, the blossom festivals, Mount Fuji, and, of course, things like the bullet train—far beyond any technology Mill Valley was ever going to be home to.

After a few minutes of chatting back and forth, Hope stopped. She sat there with kind of a funny look on her face.

Will asked if he'd said something wrong, and she said, "Nope, it's just, whenever we talk, you seem really interested in hearing about other people and their lives, but you don't spend much time talking about yourself. You're kinda different that way."

Will shrugged and carried on. "How about your brother? He's back at school, right? He's not in any of my classes. He doing OK?"

Hope leaned back in her chair.

"That's why I haven't been around much since we've been back. I've been helping William a lot at home. He's kind of struggling.

"He's a great brother, and I love him so much. It's been pretty rough for the last few years, though. As you know, he has some issues— speech and balance mostly. He gets by, but boy oh boy, other kids just don't seem to get it."

Hope explained that about three weeks before she and William were born, their mother was in a car accident.

"Another car blew a stop sign or something, and my mom ran up on the curb and hit a tree. The other driver took off, and there was a whole police thing, but it never went anywhere.

"Anyway, my mom went to the hospital, and there were some serious complications. Things looked touch-and-go for both William and me.

"My name was going to be Abigail, and William was supposed to be Benjamin. I'm sure my parents had gone looking for baby names but didn't make it past the first two letters of the alphabet," Hope laughed.

"Anyway, my mom changed her mind and said to my dad, *I'd like to name them something we have and something they'll need—Hope and Will.*'

"We arrived, and everything looked OK. A couple of years later, though, William wasn't progressing as expected—at the same rate as me, at least. Doctors suspect he suffered a minor brain injury in the car accident."

***

It was about a month after Hope's return to Valley View when, one night at dinner, Will added to his list.

"I'm thankful for a friend I've made at school."

"OK? I'm interested."

"Her name is Hope. I met her at the fair—not this August, but the year before. Anyhow, something's happening. I don't know what, but it sure feels like something."

Shadows Of Hiroshima

The final bell rang as the remaining few students shuffled into English Comp for the last class before lunch.

A kid named Oliver, who performed a stand-up routine at the previous year's talent show, announced he had a question.

"What do you do if life hands you melons?"

Everyone waited.

"Well, first of all, find out if you're dyslexic."

It took a few seconds, but he got the laugh he'd hoped for.

The class was still chuckling as Mr. Paulson stepped in from the hallway.

"All right, sounds like we're having some fun! Love it!" he said in his thick Irish accent.

"Now, let's get to it! I've graded your assignments, and today we are going to have four lucky contestants read their short stories to the class. I've picked these stories specifically because they contain components that fit in nicely with the lesson plan we've been working from.

"So, I'm going to start by discussing just that. By the way, Will and Hope, you two will read first. Then we'll take a wee break to critique, and Luke and Sydney will go next.

"I have to say, class—you turned in some very nice assignments. Excellent work!"

After hearing his name, the blood rushed to Will's face. He considered making a run for the door.

Hope, sitting a couple of rows over, glanced at him—slunked down in his desk.

"What I want to discuss today are little tricks we can employ in our writing to lead the reader on a wee journey.

"We never want to deliberately confuse the reader, but we do want to present an opportunity for the reader to discover something. 'Easter eggs' is the term, I believe.

"It can be a discovery pertaining to characters you're writing about, but it can also be a discovery the reader makes about themselves.

"You'll see what I mean when we discuss Hope's work."

Mr. Paulson pointed a finger at Hope.

"You used the term *Fat Man*. Very clever."

A few kids shifted in their seats.

"Hope's story has a very nice hook in the opening lines. She piques our interest with the term, but then immediately asserts that in her context, *Fat Man* was not at all funny. It's a lovely contradiction."

Mr. Paulson stepped over to the corner of the room, pulled out a lectern, and positioned it in front of the class.

"Are you ready, Hope?" he asked.

Hope got up from her desk, and Mr. Paulson handed her the assignment as she stepped to the front of the room.

Hope held up a picture of a Japanese man.

"The Shadows of Hiroshima," she began.

My great-grandfather, Hiroshi, was one of 180,000 civilians killed during the bombing of Hiroshima.

There was a long pause as Hope looked out at the class.

I can see I have your attention. Thank you.

Fat Man and Little Boy.

The words suggest almost a sense of humor as one's mind goes to the likes of silent movies or cartoons. But I can tell you— these two characters were anything but funny.

Fat Man and Little Boy were the names given to two atomic bombs.

We all know the story—Albert Einstein confirmed the theoretical notion that an uncontrolled nuclear chain reaction had the potential to produce a weapon of mass destruction. Thus began the process to develop 'the bomb.' It was called the Manhattan Project.

Robert J. Oppenheimer took charge.

Following the first test, on July 16, 1945, Oppenheimer quoted a line from the Hindu holy text, the Bhagavad Gita: "Now I am become Death, the destroyer of worlds."

A few weeks later, on August 6 to be exact, the atomic bomb nicknamed Little Boy detonated above the four-hundred-year-old city of Hiroshima—the seventh-largest city in Japan at the time.

Hiroshima had not been targeted during the previous three years of U.S. precision and firebombings. Eventually, though, it gained the attention of the United States. Then it was just a matter of time.

Recognizing the risk to Hiroshima, Japan forced an evacuation of approximately 125,000 people, leaving 250,000 civilians behind.

When Little Boy detonated directly above Hiroshima's Shima Hospital, it released the power of over 14,500 metric tons of TNT. A pulse of thermal energy rippled across the city, flattening twelve square kilometers. The temperature at ground zero exceeded 7,000 degrees Celsius.

A quarter of Hiroshima's residents died instantly, while another quarter died over the next days and weeks—mostly from burns.

A few days after the bombing, another nuclear device, Fat Man, was dropped on the city of Nagasaki.

The Japanese surrendered on August 15, 1945—six days later.

Hope held up another picture, pausing as she showed it to the class. The image appeared to be a dark stain on some steps.

Today in Hiroshima, there is a place called the Peace Memorial Museum. Inside the museum is an exhibit titled The Human Shadow Etched in Stone.

The exhibit—stone steps about three meters wide by two meters high—was cut from its original location outside a bank and moved to the museum. It is also known as The Human Shadow of Death.

In the past, the mark was thought to be the shadow of a forty-two-year-old woman named Mitsuno Ochi. Witness statements indicate she was seen sitting on the bank's steps prior to the blast.

The truth is, it's not a shadow at all—but rather a case where the surrounding stone was bleached white by the intense heat. The 'shadow' is actually the original color of the stone, protected by the person sitting there.

Science says complete vaporization of a body is impossible. A body exposed to even this level of radiant heat would leave behind bones and carbonized organs.

A soldier's statement indicates he moved the remains of a body from the location during a recovery operation, a few days after the blast.

As I mentioned, my great-grandfather Hiroshi also died that day.

He and my great-grandmother, Kumiko, worked a small piece of land they had inherited from Kumiko's family. They were quite successful—growing botan (peonies) for the more exclusive hotels in the city, along with vegetables Kumiko sold at her local market.

They awoke early on August 6. They planned to make the forty-five-minute train ride to Hiroshima and would arrive at 8:00 in the morning.

They were heading into the city to meet with their banker. Their intent was to acquire funds that would enable them to expand their land holdings and increase the family's wealth and status. It was Hiroshi, Kumiko, and their son, Tetsu, who were to travel to the city that day.

That morning, Hiroshi played with Tetsu while Kumiko prepared a small breakfast. They ate and were almost ready to leave—but as fortune would have it, Tetsu became increasingly fussy. He hadn't been well, so my great-grandmother Kumiko decided to stay home with her little boy.

From that twist of fate, I now live here with you, in this beautiful city.

Of course, after the bombing of Hiroshima, there was nothing. The small markets collapsed within weeks. Winter arrived.

Kumiko, now widowed, moved with Tetsu to Osaka—a city mostly untouched by bombings.

There was little in the way of support in Osaka, so they lived on the streets and eked out a living doing menial tasks for shopkeepers.

***

My parents and I vacation in Japan every summer, so I get to visit my grandfather Tetsu.

The word Tetsu translates to "iron" in English—and that he is. He grew up a strong man.

Thanks to his mother Kumiko's hard work and Tetsu's own dedication to his studies, he attended university in Osaka and went on to become an accomplished professional baseball player in Japan.

And that is my story about the Shadows of Hiroshima. But of course, I have much more to share with you. Thank you.

A few kids offered a muted applause, though most of the class sat in silence.

It was evident Hope's story had put a very human face on something everyone had read about or seen on TV or in movies. Hope's story exposed how few ever contemplated that a person in Mill Valley could be so directly connected to the event.

Mr. Paulson had been leaning against the ledge along the wall of windows. As Hope finished her story, he stepped forward, saying,

"Hope, that was very good. Informative, evocative, tragic, and inspiring—which I'd say is about all one could ask for.

"I'm sure you, as the audience, were struck when Hope referenced *Kumiko and her little boy.* For me, this specifically highlighted the juxtaposition of the story: *Little Boy* the atomic bomb, versus a little boy. Very compelling.

"A great story. Around a thousand words—a beginning, middle, and end.

"As a reader, I walk away wanting to know more about so many aspects—the shadows, the city, the culture, and this Japanese professional baseball player.

"Like, is that even a thing?"

The Bar

Hope was perched near the top of the Valley View academic leaderboard. She was a smart girl, and Will correctly assumed two things: she had the bar set pretty high, and she didn't spend much time hanging around with people who couldn't get over it.

But Will was no dummy. He recognized that being in the same classes as Hope gave him an unobstructed arena to operate in—an opportunity to impress the girl.

And since Hope's return from Japan, as a reward for stepping up his academic game, things between them seemed to be chugging along just fine.

At this exact moment, however, Will was concerned about the amount of effort—or lack thereof—he had put into the short story project. Over the last couple of weeks, he'd prioritized just about everything except getting the required number of words on paper. His paper route, karate, baseball, rugby, and track took up most of his time and energy.

Now, he sat squirming in his desk, wondering what level of embarrassment awaited him for a job half done.

Mr. Paulson stood at the lectern Hope had just vacated.

"As I was saying, creating an interesting piece of work is a process—and words matter, people! So, choose them deliberately."

"Another trick, as Will's story demonstrates, is to take words completely out of context and weave them into your work to paint a more layered and complex picture."

Hope shot a look at Will, still slunked in his desk.

"Will used the word *cannonaded*, and you'll see how he applied it in his story.

"Does anyone know the meaning of the word—or want to take a guess?" Mr. Paulson scanned the class.

"Lane," he said, pointing to a student seated at the back.

"I think it's from the olden days when navies used cannons? Not sure if I know exactly what it means, though."

"Yes!" Mr. Paulson high-fived the air. "Marvelous. Thank you, Lane!

"It's a naval term—and no, we're not talking about oranges or belly buttons. How did you arrive at that conclusion, Lane?"

"Ugh, my eight-year-old nephew was over last weekend, and I had to watch that pirate movie for, like, the millionth time!"

Another girl a couple of rows over said, "I feel your pain, girlfriend." A few kids laughed.

"Ok. Proof that knowledge comes from all kinds of places!" Mr. Paulson continued.

"Now, the dictionary meaning is 'an extended, usually heavy, discharge of artillery.'

"Will, what did you use the word to describe?"

"Um... the sun, um, coming through the window?" Will posed his answer as a question, pausing between each group of words.

His story was under a microscope, but suddenly, things didn't seem so bad. As the thought crossed his mind, he sat up just a little straighter.

Other kids in the class were obviously puzzled and intrigued.

"Yes, brilliant! You see, class?" Mr. Paulson said to a room full of quizzical faces.

"No, of course you don't see. I promise you'll understand when Will reads his story." He glanced over at Will's desk. "Well done, Will."

Will heard the words "well done" and let out a sigh of relief.

"However..."

Uh-oh. Not so fast, Will thought.

Mr. Paulson stared at Will over the reading glasses now resting on the end of his nose.

"I asked for a thousand words—with no cheating on the, the, the, the word count. And Will's work wasn't." He smirked. "Nice bit of alliteration there, even if I do say so myself."

"Will's story came in at a whopping... less than four hundred words. As such, it gave me every reason to deduct a couple of percentage points. But the story is so rich in every other aspect, I consider it to be very good work. And I'm a sucker for a love story."

He looked straight at Will and said, "Don't test me!" Then he chuckled and added, "Come on up, sir!"

He stood with Will's single handwritten page dangling like a used tissue between the thumb and forefinger of his outstretched hand.

"Now, class, listen and feel the world Will describes. Are you able to hear it, touch it, smell it, taste it, visualize it? That is the foundation of a good story—all that 'show, don't tell' stuff we discuss so often."

Will stepped up to the lectern, holding his sheet of paper with his prosthetic.

"Tough act to follow," he said, looking at Hope.

The class chuckled.

"The title of my story is *Tuesday Night*.

"*Wednesday morning, a little after 5:30, he—*"

Suddenly, a kid cut him off.

"Dude, was it Tuesday night or Wednesday morning? Make up your mind, for crap's sake!"

It was one of those guys who used to hang around with Brad. There were a couple of them in the class. Brad was long gone, but his friends weren't, and a few of them felt compelled to take up where Brad left off—birds of a feather. The other one chuckled, but no one else in the class made a sound.

As usual, Will was immune.

Mr. Paulson quickly stepped to the front of the class. "Ahhh, not cool. Not cool at all.

"Will, you'll be starting again—and this time, there will be no interruptions. Period. Understood?" He glared at the vocal student.

Her Dreams

"Tuesday Night," Will began.

Wednesday morning, a little after 5:30, he boarded a train.

Shortly before 6:00, the light rays cannonaded through the window and diffused to fill the room with soft, warm light.

He dragged his aching body up from the floor and plopped onto the bench. Still disoriented from last night's drink, he flopped down on the waxy leather seat, grasping his pounding head.

Soon, he heard a knock at the door.

He staggered over, fumbled with the latch, and slid the door back.

Standing before him was a woman.

It may have been the stench of stale smoke and old drink that made her back away—or the sight of dried blood on his chin and neck, his reward for falling in a drunken stupor the night before.

She turned and scurried off down the hall. "Hey! Where the hell are you going?" echoed as she stepped off the train.

He knew she'd be back, and it wasn't long before he heard tapping.

He slid the compartment door open.

She held two cups of coffee and carried a paper bag under her arm.

A look of sadness and traces of tears were etched on her face.

Her black hair, with just a few strands of gray, hung neatly just above her shoulders. Her overcoat, cinched tightly around her waist, indicated a shapely figure. She had a young, soft complexion—if not just a bit tired.

It would be hard to believe, should she confess to being forty-eight.

She sidestepped him and moved into the compartment.

The sun had warmed the small room, and she almost felt some sense of relief, sitting, watching the dust particles dance ever so slowly in the beams of light falling on the tired and stained linoleum floor.

She dug into the paper bag and brought out pastries, laying them on a napkin she spread between her husband and herself.

She sipped her coffee slowly, silently, while handing him the other.

Rising, she filled the small sink and soaked some paper towels.

She was cleaning him up as the train slowly pulled away.

Soon they would be back at their home—with their kids, their business, and her dreams, which she could only wish would one day come true.

***

"What does this say to you?" Mr. Paulson was back at the lectern, addressing the class. Will had returned to his seat.

A girl sitting a couple of seats from the back offered, "Sadness."

"Thank you," he said, pointing and nodding at the girl. "And yes, does it ever!

"Personally, I could feel the sadness—not just in the characters, but also in the 'tired and stained linoleum floor'; the kids out there somewhere, living with their conflicted parents; the unfulfilled dreams. I could smell the coffee. I could see those dust particles dancing in the air.

"Well done, Will."

Will remained quiet, thankful he'd dodged a bullet.

Mr. Paulson carried on with the lesson, and when the class ended, the students dispersed into the hallway. Hope hung back to chat with a friend. Will took off down the hall.

He dropped his books in his locker, grabbed his lunch, and joined Mickey in the cafeteria.

A couple of minutes later, Hope walked in with William.

"Holy crap, Will! You wrote that?" Hope said as she and her brother sat down. "Hey, Mick.

"Oh my God! He started telling us about your story, and you were slouching down in your desk. What's your problem, man? It was so good." Hope was spreading her lunch on the table.

"You've got a tough choice ahead of you, Will—pro baseball player, karate sensei, or famous author. You're gonna have a struggle making up your mind, my friend."

"I wasn't sure if it was because he liked it or if he was going to say, 'This is an example of what not to do!'" Will said.

"I knew it was too short, but I've just been so busy with stuff."

"You should have heard Hope's story, Mick. Absolutely had everyone in the palm of her hand.

"I'd love to see Japan one day," he added. "It sounds like such an amazing culture. I'd love to see 'the shadows.'"

"I think that can be arranged," Hope said as she dug through her backpack.

***

During one Wednesday spare, Will told Hope about his accident—explaining that was how his dad died. That he had one grandparent on the scene, Big O, and he was in a seniors' home. He explained that Big O was an interesting guy and, since Will was a little kid, he'd taught him a lot about baseball: rules and where players came from and stuff.

Hope was a fan and could hold her own in any discussion about the game.

"You watch," she said. "One day, there will be Japanese players here dominating this league beyond your dreams."

It was always fascinating for Will to listen as Hope talked about her family's history—especially her grandpa immigrating to a new country.

Hope played piano, and though she didn't exactly say so, Will figured she was quite good. She divulged that she took lessons twice a week before school started.

Because the subject of music came up, Will went on a rambling dissertation about music in his home.

"My mom is crazy for music, and she's always walking around the house singing. She bought me a used guitar for Christmas a couple of years ago, and she also gave me my dad's harmonica. Now I'm forced to play songs she simply will not stop singing. And if I ever make the mistake of asking her about a song, she goes full Wikipedia on me—so I gotta be careful, or I'm up 'til midnight."

"Huh. A one-armed guitar player. Name me a song," Hope said curiously.

"Last weekend, it was one by that big guy with the thick glasses—always wears pink? Can't remember his name—you know, he was huge a while back.

"Anyway, now I've got the tune stuck in my head—and it's driving me nuts! It's easy chords, and my mom loves it when I sing it—though she has the bar set pretty low!"

"Oh yeah, I know the guy. Was it his song about, like, 'being a friend' or something?" Hope said.

"Yeah, yeah. That's it!"

"Oh my God, Will. I am so going to enjoy watching you in the talent show this June!"

"Right. Are you nuts?" Will was laughing. "I'd say there is about a zero percent chance I'd be singing that song in front of a single human, let alone a theater full of people. I mean, seriously, you know how the song goes, right?

"There's a line that says, 'I can lend you a hand.'"

Will held up his left arm.

"Now, I have a great sense of humor, but I am not gonna sing that song and watch everyone start avoiding eye contact and shuffling their feet!"

"Don't worry, I'll be there," Hope replied.

Huh, Will thought, *twice she's done that.*

Sukiyaki

One Thursday after school, Will was standing in front of the trophy case, waiting for Mickey. Hope's reflection appeared in the glass. William was waiting in the foyer near the front door.

"Hey, Will. I have to run, my mom is waiting out front, but can I call you later?" Hope held out a textbook and a piece of paper for Will to write his number on.

"Um, sure." Completely caught off guard, Will wrote down his number. "Papers, then karate. I should be home around 6:30."

Hope turned and left, just as Mickey came bounding up the stairs.

"Something's up, Mick," Will said as they retrieved their bikes from the racks out front.

He filled Mickey in on the details as they rode to the start of Will's paper route. A fist bump, then Mickey made the turn for home, and Will loaded his paper sack from the drop box.

Just over sixty papers usually took Will about thirty-five minutes. Every house got one—a paper with local news and stuffed with flyers from shops and grocery stores on both sides of the river. This was the paper that featured Will's baseball pictures. He had five copies.

Once he flung his last paper onto someone's driveway, he made a beeline to the rec center. His gi and obi hung in a closet in the dojo.

Will had been helping with the kids' class for over two years. It was clear teaching really helped him improve his own karate skills.

This term, he was working on the kata *Shi Ho Hai* with five green belt karateka. The kata was one of his favorites.

Standing in front of the kids, he wove the meaning of karate and the history of *Shi Ho Hai* together. The kids seemed to love it.

"We all know karate means 'empty hand,' right?"

Will held up his right hand. "*Kara* means empty, and *te* means hand." Will looked at his left arm stump.

"Oops, sorry about that," Will laughed. "Well, just use your imagination.

"Anyway, this kata, *Shi Ho Hai,* translates as 'fighting to the four directions,' and it dates back to 1828 when it was demonstrated to Chinese dignitaries visiting the Royal Court of Okinawa."

Will explained the kata represents the movement that took karate from its birthplace to the four corners of the world.

The history of karate fascinated Will. It wasn't lost on him that the martial art he both learned and taught was a centuries-old discipline he himself was continuing to spread.

Will walked through the steps of the kata slowly.

"It's all hip torque," he said to the young students.

"If you are properly grounded, all the power of your punches is transferred right here." He touched the first two knuckles of his fist.

As he demonstrated a punch, his obi swung wildly.

The kids were completely in awe of their one-handed *Sempai* when he closed the kata with an *uraken-uchi,* a powerful back-of-the-fist strike, and a *kiai.*

***

Joey greeted Will as he was putting his bike in the shed. After a quick wrestle, they both charged up the stairs and into the kitchen.

A pot bubbled away on the stovetop, and the house smelled absolutely amazing.

"What in the heck is that?" Will asked.

His mom checked the rice cooker's timer and adjusted the burner on the stove.

"Gumbo. You'll love it."

Later they sat quietly at the dining room table—holding hands—until Will blurted, "OK, geez Mom, enough with the hand-holding, I'm freakin' starving!"

Round one was over. After a reload, Will walked back in from the kitchen with a full plate.

"Whoever invented this is a genius—especially considering all my people could come up with was a hamburger."

His mom laughed. "Early eighteenth-century cuisine influenced by Caribbeans, the French, Spanish, and Germans, along with the Native American Choctaw people and African slaves.

"In many African countries, the word for okra is *gombo*, so I'm saying they get most of the credit!"

"So, my friend Hope caught me after school and said she'd give me a call tonight to talk about 'something,'" Will said, using air quotes. "She's going back to Japan this summer.

"And, oh wow, you should have heard the story she wrote for English Comp. Do you know about the Shadows of Hiroshima?"

Will's mom walked into the living room and put a 45 on the turntable.

"This song was a huge hit when I was a kid."

Notes from what sounded like a wooden instrument started, then the first line of *Ue o Muite Arukō* began. They sat in silence, listening to *Kyu Sakamoto*.

"It's called *Sukiyaki*," Will's mom said as the artist whistled the final few bars and the song wound down. "I wonder what it means?"

"So, you kinda like this girl?"

"Um, yeah, kinda! I told you I met her at the fair, right? Like, a year and a half ago, but I think she's finally falling victim to my charms!"

Will wasn't trying to hide his excitement—he couldn't possibly.

"She said she'd call after dinner, and I'm thinking it's fifty-fifty whether I'm cool or I barf on the phone."

Will's mom laughed. "You'll be fine.

"Ask her to come for dinner," Will's mom said as they carried their plates into the kitchen.

"If the call lasts more than ten seconds, I just might do that. I'll tell her we have some Japanese music from the middle of the last century, when my mom was in school, and we need it translated."

"You're a brat!"

They were almost done cleaning up when the phone rang.

"Go!" She gave him a shove on the shoulder, then snapped a towel at his backside. Will grabbed the portable phone off its cradle and danced out of the kitchen.

Has Beans

Will was sitting in a downtown Mill Valley coffee shop. It was Saturday afternoon.

Music memorabilia spanning the last thirty years adorned the walls. Unique instruments and headshots signed by the famous—and almost famous—hung alongside autographed on-stage photos of performers surrounded by massive speakers, lights, and pyrotechnics.

Every sheet-music-plastered table was covered with a thick glass top. Menu items were named after iconic hits of the past, and an eclectic mix of music played. You were unlikely to be able to *name that tune*, though you knew you'd heard the songs somewhere.

This was the funky little venue *Has Beans*. The two owners were renowned for having recorded a couple of tunes that got some radio play a couple of decades earlier.

Hope was now three-and-a-half minutes late, and Will was starting to sweat. He didn't want to get caught craning his neck looking for her, but he couldn't seem to peel his eyes off the entrance.

He surreptitiously sniffed his armpit, grimaced, then cupped his hand in front of his mouth and breathed in through his nose.

Well, at least that's OK, he thought.

Then he looked up, and she was coming through the door. Glasses a bit crooked, arms full of books—just freakin' beautiful.

Will had arrived at *Has Beans* an ambitious thirty-five minutes early and jockeyed from table to table, finally securing a four-seater in a back corner. Hope didn't see him at first, and Will watched her for a second, noticing just a fleeting look of disappointment as she scanned left and right. When she finally spotted him, she broke into a huge smile and hurried toward the table.

"So, what? You just pulled off a heist at the library?" Will chuckled.

"Nice one," Hope said, "but you won't be laughing when you see how much homework I've got—and I'm buying—so, what'll it be?"

Massive steaming cups of rich brown latte sat in front of them, along with cookies the size of small dinner plates. They had binders and books open on the table, with more books piled on the chairs and the table beside them. No one minded. *Has Beans* was one of those places—always busy with come-and-go traffic but never more than half-full throughout the day.

The phone call on Thursday only lasted about five minutes. They planned the "have coffee" part of the afternoon—so far, so good.

Before they said goodbye, Will summoned about one hundred and fifty percent of all the nerve he could muster and asked Hope if she'd like to come over for dinner afterward.

When he told Mickey the details on Friday morning, it struck him that she said "sure" before he actually got the question out of his mouth.

Their 1:30 coffee evolved into a three hour study session, which was followed by a walk back to Will's place.

"Finally, the girl from the fair," Will's mom expressed what a pleasure it was to meet Hope, and gave her a wink. Will cringed at his mom, and he and Hope disappeared into the living room.

After checking out the vinyl collection for a while, Hope went back to the kitchen.

"Fish tacos are my absolute favorite! What can I do to help?"

Plates, bowls, and spice jars were staged on the kitchen countertop. A cast-iron pan of avocado oil on the stovetop was giving off a buttery aroma as the oil roiled in the pan. This was the assembly line supporting the evening's menu.

"Two things! We're doing chunks of cod in breadcrumbs, but it'd be great if you could jazz them up a bit." Will's mom nodded at the spices.

"Oh, and Hope, later, I need you to translate a piece of music for us."

"Glad to!" Hope confidently took charge of her assigned task—milk, egg, breadcrumbs, plate, repeat—and Will's mom floated each piece of fish in the hot oil.

Will set the table and topped up Joey's water dish.

Between Hope, Will, his mom, and Joey, they erased any evidence of fish tacos, then did some serious damage to a tub of Rocky Road.

After dinner, they hung out in the living room, talking for a while, then Will's mom put on *Sukiyaki*.

Hope listened intently, bowing her head as the musical story unfolded. Her eyes glistened. "Yes, I know this very well. I listened to this song for days after my grandmother died—my dad's mom.

"The song can be interpreted a few different ways," she said.

"The original title is *Ue o Muite Arukō*, which in English means 'I look up as I walk.' Most people think of it as a beautiful ballad about lost love. In the song, he is saying, 'I look up as I walk, so my tears won't fall,' though it's not a love song at all."

Will's mom was surprised. "Really?"

Hope explained the intent behind the song as if she could write a book on the subject.

"The song was actually written as a protest over a security treaty between Japan and the U.S."

She told Will and his mom *Kyu Sakamoto* was expressing how frustrated and dejected he was because the *Anpo* protests failed to sway the Japanese government. Despite weeks of voicing objections, tens of thousands of Japanese citizens could not stop the government from entering the treaty.

She explained that the treaty offered Japan protection against Asia-Pacific aggressors, but they had to concede huge land masses on Okinawa to the U.S. military as compensation. And how, since the signing of the treaty, there have been many horrendous consequences of having a U.S. military base on Japanese soil.

"It's so funny to have it renamed *Sukiyaki* for North American audiences. It would be kind of like calling *Let It Be* 'Beef Stew' just because it was being played in Japan," Hope chuckled. "Can we listen to it again, please?"

"I'd love to," Will's mom restarted the turntable.

"You guys put on what you want," she added as she picked up a gardening book from the coffee table. "I'm going to get scientific about the garden this year, and plants are going in soon!"

She left the living room to Will and Hope.

Hope convinced Will to get his guitar, and he did his best with *Jimmy Buffett's Changes in Latitudes, Changes in Attitudes*.

"It's kind of you, isn't it, Will?"

"What d'ya' mean?" Will asked.

Hope gave him a most intense look as she nodded her head. "You don't seem to spend much time looking backward."

Will shrugged. "You know what I always say—only now matters."

***

They dropped Hope off at her house a bit after 11:00, and Will hopped back in the car.

"Nice girl, Will."

"Yeah."

His mom drove for a couple of minutes in silence, then said, "You want to know something?"

"What?"

"Trust me, that girl likes you a lot."

Will just smiled as he looked out the window.

Talent Show

It was nearing the end of the school year, and Hope and Will were an item.

They spent a lot of time together. Most of it revolved around school projects, but whatever the reason, they seemed to be at each other's houses every weekend.

At dinner one night, Will's mom asked, "Going steady?"

Will laughed. "Yeah, right, Mom. By the way, the last century called—they'd like their words back!

"We're just tight, that's all. She's nice. I like her a lot."

"Me too," his mom replied.

Later, in his room, Will sat at his desk. He wasn't reading or looking at his cards—he was just sitting there, thinking.

A lot had changed, and a lot had stayed the same. His right-hand glove was in its home, resting on top of his dresser. His few karate medals still dangled from the bookshelf.

He opened his desk drawer, retrieved the box of collectibles, withdrew the piece of paper, and unfolded it.

One for three, he thought. *So far.*

Things were looking good for Will. He lived up to the "try-hard" promise he made his mom, and every indication was his marks would show it. The girl of his dreams watched most of his baseball games this season, and in a few weeks he and Mickey would be trying out for the summer all-star baseball team.

And with only two weeks to go at school, all that was left were a couple of finals and the talent show.

The show was an annual event held at the Royal Theater in the older section of downtown. The Saturday afternoon event acted as an unofficial wrap-up to the school year for the three local high schools.

Each year they mixed their talent pools together—acts had a ten-or-fifteen-minute window on stage, and the performances ran from morning to evening.

There was always a great turnout for the show. Parents and siblings showed up to watch kids in their time slot and usually stayed for an act or two on either side. Even the local radio station broadcasted some of the event, which prompted locals to drop by and enjoy the by-donation show.

Will, Hope, and Mickey were booked for 2:30.

Will had argued strongly against the "friend" song for the obvious reason he explained to Hope.

One of the songs they did settle on came from a discussion the three of them had one Sunday afternoon while they were hanging out in Will's living room.

"I think it's perfect, and there's a funny story about this song," Will argued.

"You sound like your mom!" Hope said.

"I heard that!" Will's mom called from the kitchen, laughing.

"Oh my God, I do! It's genetic! Thanks a lot, Mom!"

***

The program schedule billed them as *W.H.A.M.*

Will, Hope, and Mickey walked onto the stage for their performance, pretty sure there was a lawsuit pending.

"Please join in!" Mickey said, and a couple of beats later, Will started strumming left-handed with his prosthetic, while he worked the frets with his right hand.

The three of them belted out the lyrics, clapping and stomping, and within seconds, the whole audience was involved. There were more than a couple of blips, but most people didn't actually know what the song was supposed to sound like—or if they did, they didn't mind the blips.

The trio blended a couple of short numbers together, then left the stage with applause ringing in their ears. But that was only part one of what Will signed up for. Will also put his name on the list to perform a monologue, so, in the wings, he handed Hope his guitar and went back on stage.

The stage crew removed the excess equipment, and Will stood alone at a single mic stand with a spotlight beaming down.

"Hi, my name is Will Williams. I go to Valley View."

A few people in the crowd hooted or whistled.

"Today, I'd like to share a story with you. It's about a day in the life."

No cue cards—Will was winging it.

It was a warm summer evening when a reasonably new SUV pulled up out front of a nice home in an upscale neighborhood.

The driver, a guy in his mid-forties, stepped out of the vehicle and closed the door. Not gently.

He stood with his arms crossed, resting them on the roof. He was looking at his home.

Curiously, he was wearing a baseball uniform of sorts. The word "COACH" ran shoulder to shoulder across his back.

A minute passed before he seemed to resign himself to some thought, then he slowly shuffled up to the front door. With his hand on the doorknob, he paused briefly, then stepped inside.

Body language says a lot, and it was evident this was a man in a bit of distress. Everything about him indicated his team had probably suffered a loss which, in all likelihood, extended a string of similar outcomes.

In the front entrance, he kicked off his shoes then walked into the living room.

He stopped in the middle of the room and stood silently, head bowed, shoulders slumped, shaking his head from side to side.

After a few seconds, his wife walked in.

Not immediately picking up on his mood, she went about straightening a couple of pillows on the couch and asked, "How'd the game go?"

She pretty quickly realized something was amiss, adding, "Oh, geez, what happened, sweetie? Is everything OK?"

The man slowly lifted his head, looked at her, and said, "I gotta get some actual baseball players. Seriously. The guys I've got are about one step past hopeless. I don't know what I'm gonna do. I need some better players, and I need 'em quick."

He gnawed on his cheek for a second.

"I mean, these guys, they can't throw, they can't hit. Our pitching sucks, our relief pitching sucks worse and, and, and

turn a double play or something like that? Phfft! An absolute fantasy.

"I need better players. Better players," he said again, then with just a bit more desperation in his voice, he added, "That's just all there is to it."

His wife stood there looking at him.

"Well, um, wow," she cleared her throat. "Can I give you my perspective, maybe tell you what I'm thinking?"

"Honey," he said with a deer-in-the-headlights look on his face,

"Ab-so-lutely.

"You know you have been the biggest part of every bit of success I've had in this career. Since way back in the day, since coaching college, since Single-A—I mean every step of the way—you have supported me and offered me great insight, and sweetie, I completely value your opinion.

"Really, honey, you see things out there I miss, and I know it.

"So yeah, please, tell me what you're thinking. It can only help."

"Well," she said, "I think rather than wishing you had better players, you could try wishing you were a better coach."

Silence.

Will glanced to the stage's left wing. Hope was standing there with her hands clasped in front of her mouth. She looked at Will, then glanced out at the audience, then looked back at Will. Eyes wide.

A couple of moments passed. It seemed to Will as if the audience didn't quite know he was finished, or maybe they knew he was finished and didn't get it. Or, *Yikes,* he thought. *Maybe it just isn't funny.*

A low-grade level of panic rushed through Will's veins. His first, and not very helpful thought, *Now what do I do?* was quickly followed by a second, *Make a dash for the safety of the backstage.* But then he glanced to the stage's right wing and saw Mr. Paulson, the Master of Ceremonies, stepping onto the stage.

At least he was clapping and laughing.

And suddenly, the audience put the preamble and the punchline together, and there was a collective response.

As Will breathed a huge sigh of relief, Mr. Paulson stepped up to the microphone. He raised his arms asking for a moment, and, as the applause subsided, he laughingly said, "Will, that was fantastic. I loved it! What a great story!"

He turned to the audience. "And what a message! First solution is to try being better yourself. Words of wisdom on which I'm sure we can all reflect!

"And how about these kids here today—so much talent—and with a bit of *better coaching*, any one of them could make it to the big time!"

Will waved to the audience as he headed toward the wings.

Mr. Paulson introduced the next act, a juggler.

Suddenly, two tennis balls bounced off the front of the stage, and the performer quickly assured the audience, "Don't worry folks, it's only gravity!" to a smattering of laughter and applause.

Hope, Will, and Mickey grabbed seats and watched the juggler—who turned out to be darn good—finish her routine.

They sat through a couple more acts, then headed out to the lobby full of people coming and going. Will's mom was there with Hope's parents and siblings.

Booker from karate stopped for a minute. He and another karateka from the dojo had been on stage earlier doing a *bunkai* demonstration. The crowd was absolutely awestruck by their performance showing staged attacks and the corresponding defenses. They were by far the most unique act of the day.

Sensei Nic said to Will's mom, "That kid of yours has it going on, though to be honest, I've felt his punches and kicks—and anytime he tells a joke, I'm going to laugh long and loud, no matter what!" He nudged Will as he spoke.

Mickey and his dad shook hands all around, then left for the pool.

"You don't mind if we just walk home, do you?" Hope replied after Will's mom offered them a ride.

"OK with us," Hope's parents agreed.

Will's mom took the guitar and said, "Enjoy your walk and let us know what the plan is for later."

Burgers

"That'll take us about an hour walking, you know?" Will said as they stepped out of the theater.

"Know it—and looking forward to it," Hope said. The two of them made their way up 1st Avenue.

They took a right at Chester and meandered up the street.

A light breeze rippled the colorful banners hanging on lampposts and ruffled the newly outfitted maple trees lining the street. An empty coffee cup danced its way down the sidewalk.

It was a sleepy Sunday in Mill Valley. It would be another few weeks before a larger troupe of passing tourists would pay a quick visit to Mill Valley on their way to somewhere else.

A small smattering of open stores encouraged only a handful of customers into the downtown core—a half dozen cars were parked randomly.

Hope stopped after noticing something in the window of an antique store.

As they peered through the window, Hope said, "You did great, Will. I was so scared for you when people just sat there. I can't even imagine what was going through your mind."

Will chuckled. "Well, I'll tell you, in about two more seconds, I was going to start running for the rear exit!"

Hope laughed, "You are a brave man, Will. I love that about you."

Will was checking out an old baseball glove and a pair of ice skates that were part of a Sports-Through-The-Ages display.

"So, you got a couple of papers back the other day?" Hope asked as they continued walking.

"Yeah, and I did pretty well on those. Should help my final grades."

"Nice! You're happy with your year, then?" Hope asked.

"Oh, I'm having a great year! Unbelievable, actually!" Will said. He paused for a second. "Oh, you meant school."

Hope smiled.

"Yeah, you know, I think I'm pretty solid all around. I mean, I'm not you, but I did OK in Philosophy. English Comp—I figure I'm an A. Advanced Math—probably a B, surprisingly.

"And I thought History was gonna be a challenge," Will added. "It's just not my thing, and I wasn't exactly sure where I stood with the teacher, but I turned in a couple of papers a few weeks ago and got really good marks."

"It's so funny," Hope said. "Our history here is so young. We marvel at ninety-year-old buildings, while in Japan, there are restaurants that have been run by the same family for over four hundred years."

"That's just it!" Will said. "Seriously, is it history just because your grandma lived through it?

"I mean, to quote the Spanish philosopher Santayana..." Will interrupted himself and turned to look at Hope. "Wait, does that make me sound like a dork?"

"Actually, it's even worse than that." Hope was laughing.

"Well, apart from his more famous quote, 'Those who do not learn from history are doomed to repeat it,' he also said, 'History is a pack of lies about events that never happened, told by people who weren't there,' which pretty much sums up how I feel.

"I put that in an essay, and my teacher wrote *YUP!*

"Next class, we talked about how a lot of our country's history has been morphed into some kind of fairy tale. And she reminded us, of all the things we know about history, the most important one to remember is—you never know how it's going to turn out!"

"I love that," Hope said.

***

"This is where it happened. My accident." Will was holding up his left arm.

They'd walked a half dozen blocks along Chester and were standing at the traffic light at 7th Avenue.

"Oh, geez, Will. Are you OK being here?"

"Yeah, I'm good," Will said. "You know, it always feels kind of weird, but it was over four years ago now, and I get more immune to the memory of it all the time.

"I've been here quite often. My mom still works in that building," Will said, pointing kitty-corner from where they were standing.

"Hey, Will, do you want to go around the other way?" Hope pulled on his arm.

"No, it's OK. I'd actually like to tell you about it."

The light changed, and they started crossing the street.

They stood on the corner in front of Safe Harbor Insurance as Will told Hope the story again—this time from the perspective of being at the actual location. Which way he and his dad were driving. Pointing at where the truck came from and the bank it smashed into.

Eventually, they continued walking up Chester Street.

As they walked, Will told her about how things were around the house when his dad was alive, and what happened the night before the accident.

"Not sure if I ever told you this, but he apologized to me about two minutes before he died. Kinda weird, eh?"

"Wow, Will. I'm really sorry," Hope said.

"It's funny though, how since then, things have been both better and worse."

"What do you mean?" Hope asked.

"Well, my dad had problems, and I think most of them were because, when he was a kid, his dad was so abusive to him.

"I hope I'm not freaking you out?" Will added. "I know it's not a nice thing to say, but by the end, I don't think I liked my dad very much. And at the same time, I feel sorry about how things went for him, with his dad turning on him and stuff like that.

"My dad didn't treat me very well, Hope, but I'm getting to understand, he was more likely just sad. More mad at himself, than at me, my mom says.

"Anyway," Will shrugged his shoulders, "it was just a big mess. Nobody was happy—and I don't want it to sound like I'm glad he died—it's just, once he was gone, the cloud we all lived under disappeared too."

Hope remained silent as they walked.

"But I'll tell ya', once that cloud lifted, what blew in right behind it was a lot of anger. I went from being me, to being a twelve-year-old kid who couldn't tie his own shoelaces. That was tough."

Hope nodded.

"But I told you I'm seeing a counselor, right?

"She has me do this thing where I have to put stuff in buckets. I get as many good buckets as I want, but only one little bucket for crappy stuff!

"She says hanging on to things is a choice—my choice—and that there are a lot of things I don't need to keep. She's teaching me to just get rid of those, forever!

"And what's pretty cool is, I've ended up with buckets of stuff that make me feel great, and one crappy bucket with hardly anything in it.

"That one little bucket is where the bad stuff about my dad is. But he's also in the buckets of good stuff. Like, I know, on some level, he tried.

"I've got all kinds of good buckets—baseball stuff, and karate, and Big O's stories, and just so you know—I've got a big bucket full of you."

Hope smiled.

They walked on, past Has Beans, half full as usual, and made a couple of zigzags through the older part of town. They were coming to an intersection where they'd decide whose house they were going to go hang out at.

Half a block later, they walked past Jackson's store.

"I've got a funny story about the time my mom brought me here to buy a baseball glove. The guy in the store asked me if I was right-handed or left-handed, so I held up my stump and said, 'Limited options at the moment.'

"I never saw a guy sell something so quick in my life." Will laughed.

"I want you to come to Japan with me, Will," Hope blurted. "I think you'd love it, with your karate and stuff, and I know you're into those samurai movies. That history will absolutely come alive for you in Japan.

"And you read a ton of manga, right? And there's baseball in Japan, Will. A lot of baseball!" Hope was speaking a mile a minute.

"Wow, I'd love that!" Will said. "How do we make it happen?"

"Well, you know I'm leaving in a week or so, and I wanted to talk to you about that." Hope reached out and took Will's hand. "Because I might not be coming back until the fall again. And Will, it might be even later than that. My obasan—my mom's mom—isn't well, and if anything happens, a whole Japanese tradition kicks in. The mourning process goes on for weeks."

Will hummed under his breath. "Well, just so you know, if you don't come back, I'm gonna have to track you down."

"Good. I love you, Will Williams."

She reached up and kissed him.

"Oh boy, Hope, I am really gonna miss you."

"Well," she said, "you know what I always say—only now matters."

Then Hope pushed Will into the recessed front entrance of a store and kissed many more times.

***

They walked through James McKinnon park, navigated around the community gardens and through the forested greenbelt with the rusty old farm equipment, then climbed the fence into Will's backyard.

Joey came to greet them, wagging his tail furiously. Will tossed him a stick, and the three of them walked up onto the back porch and stepped into the kitchen.

"Burgers!"

CHAMPIONSHIP

All-Stars

Raj was a force at Allenby. An imposing figure at six feet five inches tall—two hundred and thirty pounds. An exotic-looking guy with dark skin and a gleaming bare scalp—a scalp usually tucked under his favorite Orioles baseball cap. He'd played in their farm system and even made it to *the show* for seven games—a long time ago.

Every year, he coached two house-league teams: Juniors, in the twelve- to fourteen-year-old age bracket, and Seniors, in the thirteen- to sixteen-year-old age bracket. Raj coached his two teams because he was looking for something. It was his mission.

Raj took Juniors playing their first year on the big diamond because he wanted to see what kind of talent was up and coming—wanted to see if there was a kid or two worth spending a bit more time on.

And he coached Seniors with the hopes of polishing a few kids up to all-star status in time for summer ball. Some years, Raj even threw his hat in the ring to coach the summer team.

Will was very fortunate when, as a twelve-year-old, he found himself practicing with Raj. There was no debate—Raj was a heck of a coach. Everyone knew: if you were lucky enough to be on his team, you were going to learn a lot about baseball.

Unfortunately, Will didn't get to play that year, but he hustled his way into Coach Raj's field of vision. Eventually, Raj had little choice but to take notice. So, for the next few seasons, he kept an eye on Will—and he saw exactly what he was looking for.

Raj drafted Will and Mickey three years in a row. Some of the other coaches started complaining that keeping those two kids together gave Raj an unfair advantage.

Raj said, "Darn rights it does, but you had your chance and didn't want anything to do with Will. So, shut-up."

And yes, Will and Mickey did learn a lot about baseball.

In late June, just as Will and Mickey were finishing up eleventh grade, the house-league baseball season came to an end.

Hope was gone. She left for Japan the weekend after the talent show. Will moped around the house for a couple of days.

Kids, Mickey and Will included, went through a few days of evaluations with hopes of playing summer ball, then waited by the phone to see if they'd made the team.

The executives for baseball in Mill Valley had their end-of-the-season meeting, and while it wasn't a unanimous decision, Raj and Jesús were selected as coaches for the summer team.

But summer ball—all-star baseball—isn't house league. Teams play to win—and organizations field teams with the expectation they will. Mill Valley, and Raj, were no exception.

The first task was to select the best of the best. After some deliberation, Raj and Jesús built a conglomeration of spring-league players from Mill Valley and the surrounding area.

Mickey was an obvious choice, and once again, Raj surprised a lot of people when he added the one-handed kid to the roster. Raj let it be known pretty quickly that there was no room for debate on his selection.

Raj had a history of getting the best out of his players. He was a guy who seemed to find the right words of encouragement and inspiration to match any situation. Words that could elevate a kid to do something not many people thought they could—that applied to Will as much as it had to any kid—ever.

In preparation for the grueling summer schedule, Raj worked the team hard—he wasn't a guy who tolerated excuses, and he didn't take crap from the players—or their parents, for that matter. It was his team, and he played to win.

And win they did.

The team played in qualifying tournaments both locally and out of town—exciting road trips filled with junk food and sleepovers in tired old motels.

They defied the odds during a winning streak that left other teams shaking their heads. They pulled off come-from-behind nail-biters and lopsided victories against far stronger, on-paper opponents. After six weeks of tournaments, the original thirty-two teams were whittled down to the final four—Mill Valley was one of them.

Safe to say, it was an unlikely story—on paper, few had given them a chance to be a finalist—but here they were all the same.

On a sunny Saturday afternoon in mid-August, Will answered a knock at his front door, and Hope literally threw herself into his arms.

Her grandmother's prognosis was excellent. After an abbreviated stay in Japan, Hope and her dad returned to Mill Valley, leaving Hope's mom, little sister, and William behind to take care of some odds and ends.

Hope and Will spent a few days catching up.

The weekend after Hope arrived, Mickey's dad loaded up the car and drove the boys to an out-of-town tournament. The four remaining teams played a round robin to decide which of them would play in a head-to-head match-up for the regional championship.

Will got back into town Sunday evening and sat at the table with his mom and Hope, telling them all about a couple of improbable wins—wins that qualified Mill Valley to host the championship game.

Will's mom doubled down on her famous sour cherry cheesecake with a chocolate mango version, and Hope slid a beautifully wrapped gift—a wakizashi sword—across the table to the now seventeen year old Will.

Scouts

Mill Valley's baseball organization did not have big-city resources, but what it did have was volunteers.

Once it was confirmed the championship game would be played at Allenby Park, it was all hands on deck, and those volunteers descended on the big diamond in force.

Raj saw to it that every kid on the team was part of that army, and within just a few days, there wasn't a speck of litter to be found or a weed left to be pulled.

New "Home" and "Away" plaques identified who would be sitting in which dugout. Bright yellow fence toppers made the tired old chain-link look proud. And if there was a surface upon which paint could be applied—it was. An ambitious amount went to the gleaming white flagpole standing just outside the center-field fence, flanking a scoreboard whose every burnt-out bulb had been replaced. They even spruced up the "THANKS BIG O" banner that ran across the bottom.

When the day of the game finally arrived—the Sunday of the first weekend in September—it came boasting another in a string of cloudless skies.

Early in the morning, a few finishing touches completed the big diamond's transformation. The grass, about the only thing still green in Mill Valley, was given a final trim. On-deck circles were laid down, along with crisply defined batter's boxes and foul lines that rolled past first and third base, carrying on to the outfield fence to join freshly painted yellow foul poles, standing in contrast to their name.

The first pitch was scheduled for 1:00 in the afternoon, and every indication was, summer's prolonged stretch of earth-baking heat would be taking quite a toll on those exposed. *Mad dogs and Englishmen*, as they say.

Early-bird spectators began arriving mid-morning, hoping to stake out prime seats in the bleachers, and well before noon, the parking lot was full, with an overflow of cars lining side streets in both directions. It wasn't only Mill Valley fans—people were coming from far and wide.

The smell of freshly cut grass, ballpark popcorn, and smoke billowing from the busy BBQ added to the excitement for the ever-growing crowd of shorts-and-T-shirt-clad spectators. Old-timers shook hands and considered whether there had ever been a game this big in Mill Valley. The newly acquainted hung around munching burgers and hot dogs, thankful for the Sunday afternoon diversion—their young kids ran around under the bleachers, making up the rules as they went.

***

Little was known about Mill Valley's opponent for the big game—they were a team from a big city a long way away. Like Mill Valley, they emerged at the top of their thirty-two-team playoff table the previous weekend.

Then they traveled hundreds of miles in a fancy, air-conditioned bus to get to what most of them called "the hick town of Mill Valley." They were spending a few nights in a new hotel downtown. Their extended stay gave them the chance to have practices in secret.

This wasn't Raj's first rodeo, and for reasons that would soon become obvious, he gave strict orders for his players to steer clear of the practice diamond.

Sure enough, early on game day, in a shocking display of psychological warfare, the visitors' bus pulled up and unloaded an arsenal of equipment that stunned the Mill Valley players—hitting nets, buckets of new balls, composite bats—you name it. And every piece of equipment, right down to their logoed bags and custom uniforms, had some kid's name printed on it. This team was big money.

***

At their final practice on Friday evening, Raj told his guys that important people would be in attendance for Sunday's game. "Scouts," he said, without adding too much more detail. That one word drew an immediate murmur from the players sprawled on the infield grass, surrounded by a storm of water bottles, gloves, and hats.

Then he walked through the group of kids in front of him. He shook every kid's hand—looked them in the eye—and told them they were good enough.

Then he said, "That's it, guys. Be here at 11:00. If you're late, you're gonna be sittin'."

No one was late.

***

Will and Mickey were going through their pre-game warm-up—soft toss back and forth—pop-ups and grounders.

They were just a couple of minutes into the drill when Will was struck by a moment straight out of *The Matrix*—it left him speechless—that is, until he walked over to where Mickey was standing and said, "What in the hell am I looking at?"

He gestured out to left field, where the visiting team was milling about. Mickey quickly spotted the reality-bender that had brought their routine to a grinding halt.

"Is that Brad?"

"Freakin' rights, it is."

"Nah, it can't be. Seriously?"

"Mick, that's definitely Brad."

"Ho-ly shit!"

As they neared the 1:00 game time, Coach Raj took his team into the shade of their dugout for some pre-game motivation.

The kids took in every word—though they also watched as the color-coordinated visitors finished a series of precision drills—each designed to strike fear into the hearts of their hosts.

It may have been working.

Will's eyes wandered over to the beaten-up equipment bag sitting in the dust at the end of his dugout. Then he looked up and down the bench.

Each player on the Mill Valley team had been given a brand-new All-Stars hat for their playoff run. That was it.

For this game, they were once again wearing the best of the used sets of uniforms the coaches could find in the clubhouse. For some reason, there were two number fours—a piece of black tape turned one of them into a fourteen. Will's mom had to sew three buttons onto his jersey.

Mill Valley had surprised its way into this championship game, and by every appearance, they were the clear underdog.

Dying Quail

The crowd buzzed with anticipation as the game's preliminaries got underway. There were a few minutes of administrative yakety-yak, and the obligatory ceremonial first pitch was thrown. Then the crowd stood to sing the song—as they hit the high notes, a collective cheer rang out, and the game began.

And it was a nail-biter.

Both teams were hitting, there were close plays on the bases, and through the first few innings, the teams were desperately evenly matched.

As predicted, the late afternoon mercury was on the rise, and so was the tension in the crowd. Yet, despite the sweltering heat, there was absolutely no chance anyone in the stands was going anywhere—nor were the spectators leaning, with rapt interest, against fences all around the park.

Then, in the top of the fourth, Mill Valley found itself in a bit of trouble when the visitors rallied and took a two-run lead. The locals wondered if those competitive early innings had been too good to be true.

But in the bottom of that same fourth inning, Mill Valley got a couple of runners aboard. Will stepped up to the plate, and Coach Raj gave the hit-and-run sign. On the first pitch, Will swung away and nailed a grounder that surprised the shortstop. Both runners advanced safely, and Will easily beat the late throw to first.

Now the bases were loaded, and by the time the visitors recorded the third out, Mill Valley had battled back and taken a one-run lead.

Will was having a great game. He started at first base, which was routine for him. The crowd, though, was more than impressed watching the one-handed kid make clutch plays—scooping the ball out of the dirt on a couple of errant throws.

That guy from the other team—Ho-ly Shit! Brad—never made it as far as first, and Will, for good reason, considered it absolute proof there is a God.

In the top of the fifth inning, as Will was heading out to take his spot at first, Raj stopped him. "Hey Will, I want ya' to go play right field. Hopefully, nothin' too exciting happens out there, and ya' can have a bit of a breather. I'm pretty sure I'm gonna need ya' to step up later."

At certain levels of ball, right field is where they send players labeled "not quite as good," but Will knew many games were decided on late-inning dying-quail hits to right field—the kind of hit that fades away from an outstretched glove while a heartbreaking run crosses the plate. Big O had schooled Will on that when he was just a little kid.

So, Will believed you had to take the right field position very seriously. And he believed Coach Raj put him there not despite his abilities, but because of them.

The visiting team went to bat, and Tommy, the Mill Valley pitcher, got into a duel with the first two batters. It took at least a dozen pitches, but eventually, he retired them both.

The third batter hit a pop fly toward right field that never threatened to do anything—that is to say, it would have been caught by any player standing out there, good or otherwise.

The ball hung lazily against the pale blue sky as Will positioned himself under it, having hardly moved more than a few steps. He waved and called off encroaching players.

"Mine! Mine! Will's ball!" and—thud—it was in his glove.

Right you are, Coach. Nothing too exciting while I'm out here, he thought as he jogged back to the dugout.

But he was wrong. The drama was coming.

Tommy dug deep and shut down the visitors in the top of the sixth—three up and three down—another dozen pitches.

When Will stepped up to the plate again in the bottom of the inning, there were two out and the bases were empty. It was one heck of a battle at the plate, but eventually, he drew a full-count walk.

Then Mickey stepped into the batter's box.

Coach Raj, leaning against the end of the dugout, touched the brim of his cap, his ear, and his sleeve—the steal sign. On the first pitch, Will slid into second, barely beating the catcher's throw.

On the next pitch, Mickey swatted a change-up into shallow center field. As cheers erupted from the crowd, Will crossed the plate, scoring his team's final run.

Will pointed at Mickey, standing safely on first base. Mickey pointed back at Will. They would relive that hit—giving their team a two-run lead—many times over the years.

When Tommy took the mound again in the top of the seventh—the final inning—he had a two-run lead to work with.

Very quickly, the lead was cut in half.

The first batter doubled to deep left field, advanced to third on a fielder's choice, then scored on a sacrifice fly to center.

With two outs and the bases empty, it still looked like Tommy would be able to finish things off—but things quickly unraveled.

Two more batters made it to first—one on a little flare over the shortstop's head, the other on a walk.

The walk told Raj that Tommy had thrown his limit for the day. He'd just faced the top of the order, and they both got on base. Tommy had simply run out of gas. He was succumbing to the stifling heat—Raj, along with everyone else, could see it.

So, with the tying run in scoring position and the go-ahead run on first, Coach Raj figured he'd better make a change. He stepped away from his spot beside the dugout, shouted, "Time, Blue," then pointed to right field, signaling Will to come in.

Once called upon, Will allowed himself one moment of trepidation, then started walking, thinking as he went, *Whichever way this goes, it's going that way because of me.*

He met Tommy heading out to take over in right field. They exchanged a few words and touched gloves. Will reflected on the blackened **W O W** burned into the thumb edge of his glove.

"Wow is right," he mumbled, giving his head a little shake.

As Will strode into the infield, he looked down at the ragged and torn toes of his cleats. The black tape he'd looped around the instep was barely holding things together. A prophecy, he hoped.

He met his coach standing between the mound and the first-base foul line. Raj just stood there looking at Will, arms folded. He didn't say a word.

The umpire had taken the pitching change as an opportunity to saunter to the backstop and retrieve a supply of new balls. Now, he started a slow walk toward Will and his coach.

Raj kind of grinned at Will. He nodded a few times, chuckled, then put the ball in Will's glove, turned, and headed back to the dugout.

They Had History

Then Will did something uncharacteristic—he allowed himself to be distracted for a moment.

He looked into the stands and caught her eye. Hope. His added motivation. He grinned and gave her a slight nod—she tilted her head and smiled.

"OK, lover boy, get your head back in the game," Will muttered to no one in particular.

He held up the ball Raj had put in his glove, turned it around a couple of times, then lobbed it underhand to Mickey. Mickey handed it to the ump, who was walking back to his place behind the plate. The ump fished a new ball out of his ball bag and flipped it to Will.

They call it a pearl. A brand-new ball—gleaming white leather, crimson red stitches. Unblemished. Will seriously hoped he could keep it that way.

Anyone who has ever spent time on the mound knows, it can be a pretty special place. You may be called upon for a simple one-and-done, perhaps a significant contribution in its own right. Or, optimistically, an extended amount of time there will allow you to bask in the light of a great accomplishment. Truth be told, though, you might just as easily end up with a heartbreak that'll keep you up all night. It's a haunting reality, and one that holds true regardless of your age.

By this point in the game, the mound had been tramped down to a fine, powdery dust. Will kicked a bit of loose dirt into the depression in front of the pitcher's rubber and, though to no avail, made an effort to pack it down.

His ears buzzed with the hum of energized fans all around the park, eager to witness what fate would throw at this one-handed baseball player. Catcalls rang out from the opposing dugout.

He was in two worlds. You couldn't tell by looking at him, but with each heartbeat, he vacillated between enjoying the moment and completely freaking out.

Finally, he straddled the rubber and stood in absolute stillness against the shimmering heat of the day. He cradled his glove on the stump of his arm, set his shoulders, and in an instant, he felt nothing at all.

The next batter was waiting. The kid was a solid player, someone who could do real damage in a situation like this. He already had a hit in the game. As he stepped into the batter's box, someone from his dugout yelled, "That's the go-ahead run on first!"

Nope, Will thought. *Absolutely no way I'm letting that happen.*

Will, the eternal optimist.

As the game situation certainly suggested, securing a win was a long way from being reality. With runners on first and second, and two out, Mill Valley's one-run lead did not offer much of a margin for error.

The ump pointed at Will and said, "Play," and the drama continued.

Will threw two pitches—a fastball away, then a slider that sailed on him a bit. Very quickly, he was behind 2 and 0. He followed those pitches with a strike, then threw another ball before finally giving up a walk that loaded the bases.

An almost imperceptible whisper of defeat washed over Will—a sliver of a moment in which his head and shoulders sagged.

It was doubtful anyone even noticed. Except for Hope.

She'd never seen anything but Will's absolute confidence, and this foreign moment of uncertainty was so new, it scared her. She studied Will intensely for a second or two, and *poof*—just as quickly as it had appeared, it was gone.

She saw who was standing in the on-deck circle—and she knew—it was payback time.

There was no denying Will really wanted the last guy. He could have ended the game with Brad standing on-deck—sweet justice. And had Will done so, none of what was about to happen next would happen at all. But apparently, that wasn't meant to be.

Brad, his team's clean-up hitter, walked slowly toward home plate. Will watched every step he took. He didn't take his eyes off him for a second. To say they had history was an understatement.

Here was the guy who had called Will *Lefty* from the very first day of middle school.

Will kept any reaction to the *Lefty* taunts in check. His strategy was to make himself immune to Brad's attempts to rile him up—which, consequently, drove Brad absolutely bat-shit crazy.

Even so, it had been frustrating for Will. Still in rehab, he couldn't fight back, but in some recess of his mind, he knew, there would come a time—Brad would cross a line—there would be an opening. And when it came, Will knew he wouldn't back down.

And sure enough, they moved on to high school, and one day in the hall—Brad did the unthinkable. That was when Will stepped in.

The day of their punches-thrown, bloody-nose, torn-shirt, and black-eye battle—broken up by a teacher—and fortunately so, because Will was losing. *Getting his ass kicked* is the common term.

***

There is little question the universe has a sense of humor.

After their fight in the hallway, Brad moved away from Mill Valley— and now, two years later, the universe brought him back.

Will had a chance to settle things.

Unfinished business, just as Brad predicted.

Skull

As Brad was about to step into the batter's box, Will called, "Time."

A classic not-so-fast tactic.

Will reached down, picked up the rosin bag, tossed it up, and caught it with the back of his hand. He tossed it up again and watched as it fell to the ground in a puff of dust. He wiped his hand off on his pants, casually turned, and studied the scoreboard for a few seconds—and then it was showtime.

His first pitch was low and inside.

Mickey picked it out of the dirt and looked threateningly down to third base, chasing the runner back.

Brad chuckled.

Mickey turned and said something to the ump.

"Time!" the ump called as he pulled out his brush and tended to home plate.

Mickey tucked his mask under his arm and stepped up to meet Will on the grass in front of the mound.

Will took off his hat and wiped his brow. His hair was matted with sweat. His jersey clung to his back like wet plastic.

"Saved my ass on that one, Mick."

Mickey looked toward third base. "No kidding!" Then he glanced toward the bleachers.

"Hey, look, Will. This is kinda what you dreamt of, right? Hope's here, big game, you're pitching."

"Yeah," Will said.

"Great. Well, then don't screw it up!" Mickey started laughing as he turned and walked back behind the plate.

"Thanks, Mick. Asshole."

Will cracked a smile as he walked back up on the mound and then he glanced over at his coach.

Yup, Raj, I get it, he thought. *This is what you meant when you told me one day I'd be staring down the barrel at some kid I have a history with.*

Raj, leaning against the dugout, just watched.

Jesús nudged him. "You going out?"

"Nah. He's good."

***

Raj was viewed by some as a hard-nosed SOB. Perhaps, by some definitions, he was, but he also did things in the background that were neither seen nor heard. If he identified a kid that had some potential, he made it his goal to help the kid along.

Will was one of those kids.

It didn't surprise Raj that Will didn't want to go anywhere near Allenby after his accident, so Raj took it upon himself to get him back to the park. He dropped off a hat and schedule at Will's house.

From there, Will's mom became a co-conspirator.

***

As Will stood there on the mound, looking at Brad, he reflected on something Raj had told him.

When you're facing a batter with size and strength and talent—and Brad had all three—you counter with attitude and force. You stare them down. You be as cocky as you can be.

So, Will glared at Brad, puffed out his chest, and tried to spit, but nothing came out.

OK, Plan B, he thought. *Just throw heat. Something right down the pipe, no movement, nothing fancy.*

Mickey dropped one finger.

Perfect, Will thought.

Mickey's sign called for a fastball down the middle, a statement pitch that would tell Brad they were coming right at him. That the rivalry was back on. A continuation, of sorts, from the afternoon in the hallway.

Brad almost screwed himself into the ground on a swing and a miss.

Will followed the fastball with a change-up that Brad absolutely crushed. Fortunately, for Will, he turned on it a fraction too early, pulled it foul, and almost took the third base ump's head off.

Will followed those two pitches with a ball, and then another. Honestly, he felt one of those balls could have gone his way—could have ended things right there—but nope, the count was now 3 and 2, and with the bases loaded, Mill Valley's one-run lead was tenuous at best.

Will adjusted his compression sleeve and took a deep breath.

He rotated the ball in his hand, feeling for the seams.

He lifted his head and looked at the target—the skull Mickey painted in the pocket of his catcher's mitt the season Will returned to Allenby as an active player. They laughed about it as they sat on the bench.

"Put it right here," Mickey said, "and they are freakin' dead!"

The orange skull, now faded and worn, was exactly where Will was putting the next pitch. No doubt. He was thinking curve, and that's the sign Mickey gave him. Two fingers. Curveball.

The ball was going to come in a little high, on a trajectory just about Brad's chest height, then start to drop and curve as it drew in toward the plate. It would fall through the strike zone, and Mickey would catch it just off the back corner.

At least that was the plan.

Last Pitch

Well, they're all standing where they should be, Raj thought.

"You're good with this?" Jesús gestured out to the field.

"So long as this guy doesn't hit it where he shouldn't, we're gonna be fine," Raj said.

Brad hit for power, and everyone knew it, so no one was expecting a grounder. He wasn't going to bunt—not now, not with two strikes on him. His previous three times at the plate each indicated a huge roundhouse swing.

What Raj was counting on was Will's ability. The best-case scenario was Brad's bat didn't get anywhere near the ball.

***

Will knew his next pitch—the curveball—was in the zone the moment he let it go. It was going to drop and fade across the outside corner of the plate for strike three.

Except it didn't.

Brad swung a little late but caught just enough of it, and the ball sailed toward right field.

Mickey stood behind home plate, his body tilted impossibly to the right.

Tommy, the right fielder, was off. There was a lot of ground to cover, but he had speed. The ball was arcing to land well short of the outfield fence, but it was going to be dangerously close to the foul line.

It was one of those dying quail.

So now, at Allenby Park on this scorching Sunday afternoon, the universal force dictating the outcome of moments in a championship game had a decision to make.

Either Brad's hit would be like a firework sent skyward—bursting with colors and sparkles to the crowd's oohs and aahs—or it would fizzle out and fall silently to the ground.

Tommy tracked the ball and dove with his gloved hand outstretched. He almost had it, but the ball tipped off the end of his glove and rolled a few feet away. Sprawled on the grass, he looked on helplessly.

Brad rounded first base with his arms raised above his head. The kid on third crossed the plate, and the guy from second—the go-ahead run—was rounding third and heading for home. The visiting players charged out of their dugout.

It was one of those moments that could have been a great, significant thing. Had everything gone well for Brad, he would have had a stand-up double—maybe even a triple. He'd have knocked in two or three runs. His team would have taken a solid lead, and Mill Valley would have been in real trouble. He would have been a hero.

But it didn't happen that way.

The universe decided on the *fizzle*.

The base ump, charging down the first base foul line, came to a stop just after the ball tipped off Tommy's glove—clearly on the foul side of the line—a game of inches.

The ump stopped, straddled the line, and with arms outstretched above his head, called, "Foul!"

The ball was dead. The play was done. And what could-have-been became nothing but an insignificant little tick on the score sheet.

The ump picked up the ball and tossed it back in.

The crowd, standing and clapping, cheered Tommy's effort. He waved as he jogged back to his position in right field.

Brad took off his batting helmet and slammed it into the ground after hearing the ump's "Foul" call.

"Bullshit!" he yelled.

Then he picked up his helmet and walked back to home plate and the admonishment of the umpire.

The other runners returned to their bases.

The fielders took their positions.

Brad said, "C'mon Lefty."

A full count. Still.

The skull target.

The pitch.

***

Will's head was bowed as he stepped down from the mound. There was a buzz from the stands, but it was just noise. He strode very slowly toward the first base foul line, lifting his head slightly as Mickey's mask fell to the ground about ten feet in front of home plate.

From the corner of his eye, Will saw Coach Raj push himself off the edge of the dugout.

The umpire took a slight step back from his slot position behind the plate. He pointed his left hand at Brad and yelled, "Yes, he did! Yes, he did!" as he raised his right hand in the air, fist clenched.

Will caught Mickey as he leaped into the air a few feet in front of him. Booker, from first, was next to throw his arms around Will, then the rest of the team swarmed Mickey, Booker, and Will—most of them falling to the ground.

Gloves and hats littered the infield.

Mickey had dropped two fingers, and Will had thrown another curveball.

As they expected, Brad swung for the fence. He'd been thinking fastball—heat—so he committed much too early, leaving himself no chance to check or correct his swing to get even a piece of the ball. His effort resulted in a weak crumpling of his knees as he lost balance—his momentum proving too great.

Brad turned and walked toward his dugout, slamming his bat into the dust. He glared back over his shoulder toward the mound.

Will didn't look at him—not for even a split second.

***

A dusty gray rental vehicle stopped in front of Will's house. Two men emerged, looked up and down the street, then strolled along the cracked sidewalk lined with a few small rose bushes.

One of them stopped and nudged the other on the arm—they looked off to their right, noticing an excessively worn patch of burnt brown lawn and a piece of plywood about the size of a home plate.

Will's mom opened the front door.

"Good morning, ma'am, we spoke on the phone," one of them said with a bit of a Southern drawl.

"My name is Lenny, and this is my partner, Hiro San.

"As I mentioned, we'd like to speak with you and Will about his future plans for college and such."

***

-POST GAME WRAP-UP-

Unassisted Triple Plays

On one of Big O's visits to the house, he found Will at the dining room table struggling with math—one of those back-to-school tasks that could bring just about any pre-teen to tears.

Seeing Will's frustration, Big O decided to offer him a bit of a baseball-trivia break.

"You think that math is tough?" Big O stopped as he was walking by. "I'll tell you what's really tough—an Unassisted Triple Play...we call 'em UTPs."

He grabbed a chair.

Will couldn't put his pencil down fast enough.

"Ya' know, back in 1962, some people decided it was real important to get to the moon.

"Heck, wasn't more than ten years later and there'd already been twelve people walkin' around up there. Pretty amazing what you can do when you put your mind to it, right? They almost made it look too easy!

"Now, the first UTP, I'm talkin' modern era, was in 1909 and here we are eighty five years later and only ten other guys have made one—last one was a couple of months ago, July 8th, matter of fact.

"So there ya' go, easier to go walkin' on the moon than to get yourself a UTP!

"But you know what else, Will? You can actually make an Unassisted Triple Play without ever touching the ball."

"No way!" Will scoffed.

"Oh yeah, it's true. It ain't in the rule book in black and white, you have to know a bunch of other rules and join 'em together."

"OK, Grandpa, how exactly?" Will asked, happy for the diversion.

"Well, ya' gotta have two runners on base, and nobody out. How else could you make a triple play, right?

"Now, imagine them two runners are on first and second, and the next batter hits a towerin' pop fly that's gonna come down and land somewheres around second base.

"Well, the umpires will point up at the ball and call "Infield Fly! Batter's Out!"

"The Infield Fly Rule. Right?" Will said.

"Right you are. And when they do, the batter is Out right away and the player who gets credit for the Out, is the player who could have, according to the rules, 'Ordinarily caught the ball.' Well, it's the guy playing second of course, because he is near where the ball was gonna land.

"But the play ain't over on an Infield Fly—the ball is still alive," Big O went on.

"Now suppose the runner from first base wasn't paying attention, and he took off soon as the ball was hit, and then went right by the runner at second base?

"Well, he's Out. You can't pass another guy on the bases. And the guy playing second base is closest to the 'infraction', so he gets the second Out.

"Now, also suppose the runner that got passed is just standing there, he's not on the bag at second, he's just near it—that's important.

"Well, he's all flustered, and darned if the ball doesn't come down and hit him right on top of his head," Big O chuckled.

"Which means he is Out too. You can't interfere with a batted ball, the guy playing second base gets credit for the third Out, and an Unassisted Triple Play, and nope, he never touched the ball.

"Ain't never happened, and ain't likely too, but that's baseball!"

"Huh. Tell me another one Big O," Will said.

"Huh, nice try. Now get back to that math!" Big O said as he retreated to the kitchen to see what it was that smelled so darn good.

***

Manufactured by Amazon.ca
Acheson, AB

16635901R00109